The Case of
the Indian Curse

The Case of the Indian Curse

by Robert Newman

Atheneum 1986 *New York*

Atheneum
Macmillan Publishing Company
866 Third Avenue, New York, NY 10022

Composition by Heritage Printers, Charlotte, North Carolina
Printed and bound by Fairfield Graphics, Fairfield, Pennsylvania
Designed by Mary Ahern

10   9   8   7   6   5   4   3   2   1

Library of Congress Cataloging-in-Publication Data

Newman, Robert.
The case of the Indian curse.

SUMMARY: While Inspector Wyatt and Andrew's mother
are on their honeymoon, Andrew and Sara investigate a
mysterious statue that produces light and sound.
[1. Mystery and detective stories]   I. Title.
PZ7.N4857Casi   1986   [Fic]   85-28686
ISBN 0-689-31177-X

For John Bennett Shaw,
Dean of Holmesians, Canon of the Canon
and Most Irregular of the Irregulars
&
For Jon Lellenberg,
Warden of the Word and Guardian of the Gate.

Vivat clamor: Ludus Es Pes!

Contents

The Case of
the Indian Curse

I

Beasley

As soon as he saw Sara, Andrew knew that something was wrong. Not because she was there at the station waiting for him. She had started her own spring vacation a few days before, so she was able to be there. And not because of the way she looked, which was quite composed — actually more composed than a girl her age had a right to look when Paddington was surging with boys of every size and shape, coming home from school as Andrew was.

How did he know then? He couldn't have told you. All he would have said was that he had known Sara for some time, that they had been through a great many things together, and he *did* know. The only questions in his mind were exactly *what* was wrong and how serious it was.

Carrying his own bag so as not to have to wait for a porter, he worked his way through the crowd, surrendered his ticket at the barrier, and went on to where Sara and Fred, the Tillett coachman, were waiting.

"Hello, you two," he said.

"Hello, yourself," said Fred. "I'll take your bag."

"Thanks, Fred." Then, turning to Sara, "All right. What is it? What's wrong?"

"Coo!" said Fred. "He's not just the original boy detective. He's a blooming mind reader. How'd you know something was wrong?"

"You just guessed how. Because I'm a mind reader." He didn't mind Fred's manner, for Fred was by no means an ordinary coachman, as Sara's mother was by no means merely the Tilletts' housekeeper. She and Sara were, as a matter of fact, virtually members of the family. "Just tell me if it has anything to do with my mother."

"Why on earth should it have anything to do with your mother?"

"Well, after all, she is away."

She was more than away. She had recently married Inspector Peter Wyatt of the Metropolitan Police, and the two were on the continent on their honeymoon. Sara realized that she should have expected that this would be very much on Andrew's mind.

"No, Andrew," she said. "As far as I know, she and Peter are fine. If there's something wrong — and I'm not really sure there is — it's with Beasley."

Beasley was an old friend of theirs, a strange and interesting dealer in odds and ends with a shop on Portobello Road. They had originally met him through Wyatt.

"You must have some reason for thinking something's wrong," said Andrew reasonably.

"Well, yes. You remember Sean?"

"Who works with Beasley? Of course."

"Well, he came to the house this morning and wanted to know when Peter would be back. I said by the end of the week, and he looked upset, as if that wasn't soon enough, and asked if I was sure. When I said I was, he said he'd been to Scotland Yard and asked Sergeant Tucker, and Tucker either didn't know when they'd be back or wouldn't tell him."

"Did you ask him why he wanted to know?"

"Of course. But he didn't answer, just thanked me and left, still looking worried."

"All right," said Fred as they looked at one another. "I'm as much of a mind reader as anyone else. Let's go."

"Where?" asked Andrew.

"You know where — where you both want to go — Portobello Road."

Exchanging smiles, they followed him out to Praed Street where the Tilletts' landau waited between a hansom and a four-wheeler. Fred thanked the cabman who had been holding the horses for him, opened the door for Sara and Andrew, climbed up into the box and, shaking the reins, started south and west over toward Bayswater

Road. Traffic was light — it was getting on to teatime — and it didn't take long to get to Portobello Road.

It wasn't one of the market days, so there were no carts lining the street or crowds moving up and down it, and they were able to stop directly in front of the shop.

"Looks closed," said Fred as Sara and Andrew got out of the carriage and went over to it.

The shop did seem to be closed. They tried the door, and it was locked. The window contained most of the same oddments that had been there when they had first come to the shop and met Beasley: a brass samovar, some glass paperweights, a marble head of Napoleon, and a Turkish yataghan. They peered through the grimy glass, but there was no light or sign of movement inside.

The door of the adjoining shop opened and a wispy, gray-haired man came out.

"Looking for Beasley?" he asked.

"Yes."

"He's sick, hasn't been here for a couple of days. But if you come around in the morning, you'll likely catch Sean what works with him. He'll tell you how he is and where you can find him."

They thanked the man, and he went back into his shop.

"Well, there you are," said Fred. "That should make you feel better. At least now you know why Sean was upset, what he was worrying about."

"Do we?" said Sara.

"Well, of course. It's because old Beasley's sick."

"I can see him calling in a doctor if that's so," said Andrew. "But what has being sick got to do with Scotland Yard and wanting to get hold of Peter?"

2

The Face of the Destroyer

They went back to Portobello Road the next morning. Fred would have been happy to take them — he had little enough to do with Andrew's mother away — but Andrew and Sara preferred to go by themselves; so they left him grumbling about youngsters who think they know everything and can do anything they want and took a bus, a light-green Bayswater bus.

It was a raw, overcast day that so clearly meant rain or a heavy fog that Sara wore a cape and Andrew a mackintosh. But since at the moment it was merely threatening, they sat on top and up front, right over the horses. They got off at Notting Hill Gate and walked up Pembridge Road and over to the shop.

Saturdays and Sundays were Portobello's big market days, so again there wasn't much traffic along the street — no carts and only a few stalls in front of the shops. They peered in through the glass of Beasley's shop and saw a light on in back. They tried the door, found it open, and went in.

Sean appeared as soon as he heard the door. Though he was as nicely dressed as usual, his suit was a little wrinkled, as if he had not had it off in some time, and his red hair was disheveled.

"Hello, Sara. Oh, hello, Andrew," he said, shaking hands with him. "Nice to see you again."

"How's Beasley?" asked Andrew.

"How'd you know he was sick?"

They told him.

"Well, he's no better. Not at all good, as a matter of fact."

"How long has he been sick?" asked Sara.

"I'm not sure. I'd say about a week. I only noticed it four or five days ago. And it's only three days now that I've been able to get him to stay home."

"What's wrong with him?" asked Andrew.

"I don't really know. I just know he's sick, won't eat, can't seem to sleep. I've been with him most of the time, taking care of him. That's why I look this way." He indicated his wrinkled suit with distaste. "I only came into the shop for a while this morning to make sure everything was all right here."

"Have you had a doctor in?" asked Sara.

"No."

"Why not?"

"He didn't want one, said there was nothing wrong with him."

"But that's ridiculous!" said Sara. "If he's as sick as you say he is — sick enough to stay home . . . Can we see him?"

Sean hesitated a moment, then nodded.

"Yes. Why not? Actually the person I'd most like to have see him is Inspector Wyatt. But since he's not here, you're probably the next best thing. Let me just take care of a few items in back, and we'll go."

As he disappeared into the back of the shop, there was a light tapping on the window. Sara and Andrew turned. A dustman's cart, heavily built and with high sides, stood at the curb, the horse waiting patiently, head down between the shafts. The dustman himself was peering inquiringly in at the window.

"There's a dustman here who seems to want you, Sean," called Andrew.

"Is it Willie?" asked Sean from the back room.

"Willie?"

"Whispering Willie." He came out. "Yes, it is. Tell him I forgot about the bins yesterday, but they're out in the alley now."

Andrew went out and gave Sean's message to the dustman, who wore the dustman's usual costume of knee breeches with a smock and a coarse gray jacket over them. His leather fantail hat covered his head and a back flap hung down over his shoulders. He was so dusty with ashes that it was impossible to tell his age, but he was probably in his late thirties or early forties.

"Right, guv'ner," he said in a rasping, whispering voice. "I hear old Beasley's not well. True?"

"I'm afraid so."

"I know about that." He touched his throat, which was wrapped from the chin down in a dirty bandage. "Had this quinsy for months now and can't seem to shake it. Tell him Willie was asking for him, will you?"

"I'll do that," said Andrew.

He watched him take his basket from the cart and go down the alley. After pouring the ashes and rubbish from the bin into the basket, Willie lifted the basket to his shoulder, came back up the alley, and emptied it into the cart. Then, hanging the basket back on the cart, he sent the horse up the street. As he did, he raised a small horn that hung around his neck on a lanyard and blew a low, plaintive blast on it.

"Why the horn?" Andrew asked Sean, who had come out of the shop and was locking up.

"What?" Sean glanced after Willie. "Oh, because of his voice. Because he can't sing out like other dustmen. If he didn't have the horn — I think it's a boat foghorn — no one would know he was there."

That made sense to Andrew, and he nodded.

"Why did you say that if Peter Wyatt couldn't see Beasley, we were the next best thing?" asked Sara, as Sean led the way up Portobello Road.

"Well, you're friends of the inspector's, aren't you?"

"More than just friends. He's Andrew's stepfather now. But if Beasley's sick, I don't know why you want Peter to see him rather than a doctor."

Sean looked at her sideways.

"I never said I wanted the inspector to see him *instead* of a doctor. I'd like both of them to see him."

"Why?" asked Andrew.

"Why don't we wait to talk about it until after you see him?"

Andrew glanced at Sara and then nodded.

They went several blocks up Portobello Road, then turned north and went several more. What dealers throughout London call "the Road" is far from elegant, with its littered streets and its shops crowded together, but as they went further north, the neighborhood became even less attractive. They passed street after street of houses all exactly alike, not really slums, but the next thing to it, for most of the buildings needed paint and repairs of one sort or another.

Finally Sean paused opposite a row of small, semide-tached houses that, like most of those they had passed, had seen better days.

"Here we are," he said, nodding to the first house on the corner. "That's where old Beasley lives."

There was a builder's yard across the street with a board fence around it. Through the gate, you could see piles of lumber, sand, and bricks. The house next to Beasley's was even more dilapidated than his, with many of its shutters missing and those that were left hanging crookedly. It was apparently a rooming house, for there was a sign in the window stating that there were rooms for rent.

Sean led the way across the street, produced a key, unlocked the door, and went in.

"Good morning, Mr. Beasley," he called up the stairs. "It's Sean, and I've brought you some company."

Sara and Andrew followed him in. They were in a narrow, dark hallway with a flight of stairs in front of them. To their right was a parlor that looked like an annex to Beasley's shop, for it was full of furniture of all kinds and all periods, with packing cases set down wherever there was room for them. The air was musty, as if a window hadn't been opened anywhere in the house for some time.

Sean went up the stairs and opened the door of the rear bedroom.

"And how are you this morning?" he asked cheerfully.

"About the same," grunted Beasley. He looked at Sara and Andrew, who had followed Sean into the room. "What are you two doing here?" he asked angrily.

"They came to the shop, and when they heard you weren't well, they insisted on coming to see you," said Sean.

"And don't I have anything to say about that?" said Beasley. "I told you I didn't want any visitors — didn't want to see anyone at all!"

Sara and Andrew had been staring at Beasley, shocked at the way he looked. He was a big man and had always been on the heavy side, with good color and plump, pink cheeks. Now, lying there on the large, untidy bed, he looked like a shadow of himself, for he was pale, with lackluster eyes, and he had lost so much weight that he was almost thin.

"Since when have we been just anyone?" asked Sara, getting hold of herself.

"What do you think you are?"

"Friends. Andrew just came home from school yesterday, and when I asked him what he wanted to do this morning, he said he wanted to come and see you."

"That's true," said Andrew. He had been studying Beasley also, and he suddenly realized that the sick man's eyes weren't just dull. They were evasive, fearful. Beasley — who had worked closely with Peter Wyatt on so many occasions and been strong, ingenious, and unshakable — was not just frightened of something. He was terrified!

"Have you had breakfast yet?" asked Sean.

"No. And I don't want any."

"Now you stop that! You've got to eat. If you'll stay with him," he said to Sara and Andrew, "I'll go downstairs and fix something for him."

"Just some tea," said Beasley. "Don't bring me anything else because I won't eat it."

"Not eating is something new for you," said Andrew as Sean went downstairs. "I've eaten more interesting food with you in more unusual places than with anyone else I know. How long have you been sick?"

"I'm not sure. About a week, I think."

"Have you had a doctor in?" asked Sara.

"What do I need a doctor for? I know what's wrong with me."

"Do you?"

"Of course. It's the Spanish influenza. There's a lot of it around."

"I haven't heard anything about it," said Andrew. "Do you have a temperature?"

"I don't know. I haven't taken it. But I have a headache, and I'm always thirsty."

"That doesn't mean you have influenza."

"What do you know about it? Are you a doctor?"

"No, but—"

"Then why don't you mind your own blinking business?"

And pulling the blanket up, Beasley rolled over, turning his back on them. Andrew and Sara glanced at one another but didn't say anything. Andrew went over to the window, wondering if he dared open it so as to let in some fresh air but decided he'd better not. A neglected garden outside held a single, forlorn tree in the far corner. There was a brick wall on the street side of the garden, the blank wall of the house next door on the other and, across the rear, a board fence with nails projecting from the top to discourage intruders. Beyond the rear fence was some scrubby waste land that ran north to a spur of the Great Western Railway.

Beasley didn't move, but he clearly wasn't asleep because he sat up again as soon as Sean came into the room, looked at the tray he was carrying, and said, "I said just tea! Take the rest of that stuff out of here!"

"It's just toast, Mr. Beasley. And a pot of the kind of jam you've always liked."

"Well, I don't want it. Take it away!"

"No, don't!" said Sara firmly. "If he doesn't want to eat the toast, he can leave it."

"Are you starting to give orders around here?" asked Beasley irascibly.

"Yes, I am. And about time, too. Why are you being so difficult when Sean's doing everything he can to help you?"

"Did I ask him to?"

"No, you didn't. And you didn't have to because he's worried about you — just as we are. He wanted to do anything he could for you. But if you go on this way. . . ."

"Then what? You'll go away and leave me? Good!"

"I told you before, I'm not sure you have the influenza," said Andrew. "But whether you have or you haven't, I think we should get a doctor in to look at you."

"Don't you dare! I told you I don't want a doctor! If you bring one here, I'll throw things at him!"

"No, you won't — not at this doctor! Come on, Sara, Sean."

"Wait a minute!" shouted Beasley as they went out. "Come back here, you nosey, interfering brats! Sean! Sean!"

But Sean paid no attention to him and followed the two young people down the stairs.

"Well?" he said. "What do you think?"

"He may be sick," said Andrew. "He certainly looks awful. But I think mostly he's frightened — very frightened."

"You think so, too?" said Sean. "That's why I didn't want to tell you what I thought was wrong with him. I wanted to see what *you* thought."

"That's what I think, too," said Sara. "That he's terribly worried, terribly afraid of something. But if that's so, why is he against seeing a doctor?"

"Because if the doctor's any good," said Andrew, "he'll know he's not really sick. He'll know that there's something scaring him, and he'll want to know what it is."

"I think you're right," said Sean. "Was there a particular doctor you were thinking of bringing in?"

"Yes. Dr. Reeves of St. Mary's Hospital. He's a friend of Peter's, and he's heard about Beasley from Peter and from us."

"Is he the doctor who took care of the old man we

smuggled out of the house on Sherburne Square?"

"Yes."

"From what I heard, he should be able to handle anything," said Sean. "Even Beasley."

"He will," said Sara. "But he's going to ask even more questions than we have. For instance, do you have any idea what he's frightened of?"

"Yes, I think so."

"You know?"

"I wouldn't say I know, but I'll lay you a Brummagem sixpence to all of Lombard Street that that statue had something to do with it!"

"What statue's that?" asked Andrew.

"He had it in the shop about a month ago. It was an Indian statue of Kali. Do you know who that is?"

"Yes," said Andrew. "She was the wife of Shiva and was known as the Destroyer."

"And she looked it! Four arms she had. Blood on her mouth and hands, fangs like a tiger, and a necklace of skulls. Fair gave me the jimjams, she did, just to look at her."

"Where did Beasley get it?" asked Sara.

"I don't know. He wouldn't say."

"Is it still in the shop?"

"No."

"Where is it then?" asked Andrew.

"I don't know that either. He had it in the window for a while and suddenly it was gone. When I asked him what had happened to it, he told me to mind my own business."

"Maybe he sold it," said Andrew.

"No, no. I keep the books, and it would have been written down if he'd sold it. It just disappeared."

"And you think the statue had something to do with his being sick?" said Sara.

"Well, it was after he got it that he started acting scared and funny."

"Are you saying you think there was a curse on the statue?" said Sara, her eyes wide and a little frightened.

"Maybe," said Sean. "Maybe it was stolen and the priests wanted it back."

"But if it's gone, why should Beasley still be frightened?" asked Andrew.

"I don't know. Maybe he didn't give it back to them. And, even if he did, maybe they're still angry at him. All I know is that I'll give you odds that that statue had something to do with what's happening to him!"

3

Dr. Reeves

"Of course I remember you," said Dr. Reeves. "You're friends of Peter Wyatt. We met during that very strange affair with old Benedict Cortland. You went to school with his grandson, didn't you?"

"Yes, sir," said Andrew. "And I still do."

"I saw the old gentleman the other day at the club. I must say he seemed fine. And of course I heard some perfectly splendid news about Peter. Married your mother, didn't he?"

"Yes, sir."

"Well, that makes him a bit more than a friend of yours. Is he still away?"

"Yes, sir. On the continent. But they should be back very soon."

"I've been meaning to write him a note of congratulation. About time he was married. And I gather your mother is not only beautiful and a fine actress, but a wonderful woman."

"She is," said Sara emphatically. "She's the most wonderful woman I've ever known."

"Well, I'm glad to have that confirmed by someone disinterested," said Dr. Reeves, smiling. "Now, what can I do for you?"

"We wondered if you could come and look at a friend of Peter's and ours. We're very worried about him. His name's Beasley, and he doesn't live too far from here."

"Beasley. Was he the chap who winkled old Mr. Cortland out of his daughter-in-law's house by pretending it was on fire and brought him here to the hospital so I could treat him?"

"Yes, sir."

"Smart piece of work that was. I always wanted to meet him. What seems to be his trouble?"

"Well, he claims it's nothing — a touch of the Spanish influenza — and says he doesn't want to see a doctor. But we think it's a lot more than that."

"From what I know of you, I'm sure you wouldn't say that without reason. Yes, of course I'll come to see him. I've finished rounds here. Just let me give these charts and some instructions to Sister Wingate and we'll go."

It was now late in the afternoon, almost four o'clock. They had gone over to Dr. Reeves' surgery on Wimpole

Street and found that he was not going to be there that day. He was out on calls, but he would be at St. Mary's Hospital at two. Since they were not too far away, they stopped in at the British Museum, thinking they might find out something about the statue of Kali, but they discovered that there were almost no Indian artifacts there. They were all in the Indian Section of the Victoria and Albert Museum. So they had lunch in the museum's refreshment room and then went over to St. Mary's and were waiting on the second floor of the hospital when Dr. Reeves came down the corridor from the men's ward.

"All right," he said, rejoining them. "Now where is your friend Beasley?"

He nodded when they told him, led them downstairs to where his carriage was waiting, and a few minutes later they were at Beasley's house.

Sean, looking even more worried than before, let them in.

"How is he?" asked Andrew after they had introduced him to Dr. Reeves.

"Not good. In fact, I think he's even worse than he was."

"In what way?" asked Dr. Reeves.

"He's not making sense. I'm afraid he's out of his head."

"You mean he's delirious?"

"I'm not sure."

"Where is he?"

"I'll show you."

Sean led the way upstairs, and Sara and Andrew followed behind Dr. Reeves. Beasley was hunched up in one corner of the bed, not exactly sitting up, but not lying down either.

"Good afternoon, Mr. Beasley," said the doctor crisply. "I'm Dr. Reeves. We've never met, but I believe you've heard of me."

Beasley looked at him with dull, sunken eyes and muttered something.

"I'm sorry. I'm afraid I didn't hear you," said Dr. Reeves. Beasley didn't even mutter this time. He grunted.

"It would be helpful if you told me how you feel, Mr. Beasley. Do you have any particular pains? Do you have a headache, for instance?"

Beasley stared at him without saying anything. Dr. Reeves felt his forehead, bent down and looked at his eyes, then took out his stethoscope.

"I think the two of you should wait downstairs," he said to Sara and Andrew. "I won't be too long. But I'd like you to stay in case I need some help with him," he said to Sean.

"Yes, doctor," said Sean.

Dr. Reeves was listening to Beasley's chest as Sara and Andrew went out and down the stairs. In spite of the fact that there were several chairs and sofas in the parlor, it was hard to find a place to sit because there were boxes and books piled on everything. Andrew lifted a bound set of the *Proceedings of the Royal Society* off an arm-chair so that Sara could sit and sat down on a packing case himself. They waited in silence, and Andrew knew that Sara was as upset at what was happening as he was — and for the same reason. Because nothing could be more unlike the buoyant, wryly humorous, self-sufficient Beasley than the weak and frightened man they had left upstairs.

When Dr. Reeves, followed by Sean, came into the room about fifteen minutes later, he looked grave.

"What do you think, doctor?" asked Sara.

"I don't know what to think — except that I'm quite sure it's not influenza. He doesn't really have a fever — not more than a degree or two — so he's not delirious. But still he's certainly not rational. In addition to that, he seems to be frightened of something."

"That's what we thought," said Sean. "He fell asleep just before you came, and in his sleep he started saying, 'No! No, I won't! Never!'"

"He's going to be all right though, isn't he, doctor?" asked Andrew.

"I think so. I'd feel better if I could make a firm diagnosis, but it's hard to do that when he's not responsive, won't talk to me and tell me some of the things I'd like to know. However, I've written a prescription for something I'd like him to start taking immediately. Is there a chemist near who can fill it?" he asked Sean. "Or would you like me to take you back to the hospital and have the pharmacist there make it up for you?"

"There's one in Pembridge Road," said Sean. "The thing is, old Beasley shouldn't be left alone, should he?"

"No, he shouldn't."

"We'll stay with him while you take care of the prescription," said Sara. "We didn't say what time we'd be home, and anyway mother never worries when I'm with Andrew."

"That's fine, then," said Sean. "And while I'm at it, if you don't mind, I'd like to take care of a few things at the shop. But I should be back here by five."

"That will get us home in plenty of time," said Andrew. "Have you any instructions for us in the meantime, sir?" he asked the doctor.

"No. Keep him quiet, give him all the liquids he wants, and I'll stop by to see if he's any better tomorrow."

Sean and Dr. Reeves left together, and Sara and Andrew went back upstairs to Beasley's room. The fog that had been moving in since morning was getting thicker, settling down over the city and gradually obscuring the garden outside the window. Beasley, sitting up in bed, was looking at the fog with a puzzled expression.

"Sean had to go out," said Sara matter-of-factly, "but we're going to stay with you. Is there anything you'd like while we're waiting for him to get back — some tea, for instance?"

Beasley nodded. "Yes," he said. "Tea."

"I'll go make it," she said and went downstairs.

"Sean went to get you some medicine," said Andrew.

"But, in the meantime, how do you feel? Any better?"

"Maybe a little," said Beasley.

"You look and sound better. Do you know who I am?"

"Of course. Andrew."

"That's good. That's very good."

"What's good about it? Stop treating me like an invalid or a blooming idiot!"

Andrew smiled. It was the first sign they'd had of the old, normal Beasley, and it made him feel more hopeful than he'd been all day. He was still smiling when Sara came back to the room with the tea.

Sean finished printing the sign that said the shop would be closed until further notice and hung it in the window. Then, picking up the package that he had been wrapping, he closed the door and hurried off to the post office. It had been very much on his mind, for the customer to whom it was addressed was a very good customer and he was sure that Sara and Andrew would not mind if he took a few minutes to send it off to him.

As it happened, the post office was crowded and it took more than the few minutes he had thought it would. Then he went back to the chemist's. Dr. Reeves' prescription wasn't quite ready, and he had to wait there, too, but it was still only ten to five and even though the fog had gotten quite thick — the kind they called a London Particular because you couldn't find one like it anywhere else — he thought he should be back at the house by five as he had promised.

He hurried back up Portobello Road, avoiding the rare pedestrian more by instinct than sight, for by now he couldn't see more than three or four feet ahead of him in the yellowish murk that obscured everything, turning the glow of the gaslights into faintly seen, watery moons.

As he turned north and walked on, his footsteps echoing hollowly in the damp air, he marveled at how much better he felt than he had that morning, principally because of the arrival of Sara and Andrew. Until they came, he had been completely alone, not only for the physical care of Beasley, but alone in his concern about him, too. But now, that was all changed. Sara and Andrew were almost as fond of Beasley as he was. Not only that, but they had been able to do something he hadn't — bring in a doctor who could tell them if what was wrong with Beasley was physical as Beasley claimed or something else.

Sean had reached the builder's yard by now and was walking along the board fence that enclosed it. The yard was closed. It had been closed for several weeks; but as he reached the gate, he had the impression that it was slightly ajar. Had a watchman opened it? He didn't recall having seen a watchman there before, but he hadn't really paid much attention to it. He glanced across the street at the house, noticing that there was a light on in the parlor.

He hoped that he wasn't too late — that Sara and Andrew weren't getting impatient — then, as he started across the street, he heard sudden light footsteps behind him. He turned, caught a glimpse of a crouching figure coming toward him out of the fog. As he peered at it, trying to make out who or what it was, footsteps approached him from the other side. Something struck the back of his head, his knees buckled, and he pitched forward and lay still, half on the pavement and half in the gutter.

4

Terror in the Garden

"What time is it?" asked Sara.

"A quarter after five," said Andrew, looking at his watch.

"Oh. Sean's late."

"Yes, he is." He walked over to the window and looked out into the street. "The fog's gotten thicker. Maybe that held him up."

"Maybe."

They were downstairs in the cluttered parlor. Beasley had fallen asleep a short while before and they had come downstairs, afraid that their presence in the small bedroom might disturb him.

"I wonder if I should go out and look for him," Andrew said.

"It's not *that* late. If he gets here in the next half hour, we can still get home before Mum is likely to start worrying about us."

"I know. But I'm getting a little worried myself. It's not like Sean to say he'll be back by five and not be here."

"No, it's not. If you want to go look for him, go ahead. But don't stay out too long."

Putting on his hat and mackintosh, Andrew went out. Something was happening at the rooming house next door — the door was open, and people were talking and coming out — but he paid no attention to it. The truth was that although Andrew was a bit worried about Sean, he had also been finding it difficult to remain in a stuffy house all afternoon doing nothing, and he was very anxious to get out. He walked as quickly as he could over to Portobello Road and along it to Beasley's shop. It was closed, and there was a sign in the window that said it would remain closed until further notice. That meant Sean had been there. Had he been to the chemist's, too? Andrew wasn't sure exactly where that was and, remembering Sara's request that he not stay out too long, he turned and went back. There was no traffic moving at all, and he only came across two pedestrians moving cautiously through the fog. That may have been why he paused when a stout woman wrapped in a shawl and carrying a carpetbag came out of the boardinghouse next door to Beasley's. She stopped, too.

"You ain't going in there, to old Beasley's house, are you?" she asked.

"Yes, I am. Why?"

"Don't you know what's going on in there? Beasley's got the cholera!"

"Cholera?"

"Yes. About the worst sickness you can get — once you get it, you're sure to die. That's why I'm getting out of here — me and everyone else here in the house!" and she pulled the door shut and locked it.

"Who told you that, that Beasley had cholera?"

"Why, the doctor. He knocked at my door and said even though we weren't in the same house, it was still dangerous and we ought to leave and stay away until poor Mr. Beasley was taken away."

"What doctor was that? What was his name?"

"I don't know what his name was. He was dark and kind of foreign, and—" She broke off, peering at Andrew. "Wait a minute. Didn't I see you coming out of Beasley's house before?"

"Yes."

"You was in there! You probably got the cholera, too! And I been standing here talking to you! Ow-ooh!" And with a cry that was half a moan and half a screech, she went waddling off into the fog.

Andrew stared after her, then knocked on Beasley's door. Sara must have been waiting for him, for she let him in at once.

"Any sign of Sean?" she asked.

"No. He'd been at the shop — he put a notice in the

window that it was closed — but he wasn't there when I got there."

"That's strange."

"That's not all that's strange," he said, and he told her of his encounter with the woman, who was probably the landlady of the boardinghouse next door.

"Cholera!" she said. "Beasley doesn't have cholera! If Dr. Reeves had the faintest suspicion he had anything like that, he never would have let us stay here."

"Of course he wouldn't. But the man who spoke to her wasn't Dr. Reeves. We can't even be sure that he was a doctor."

"Who was he then? And why did he say it?"

"I don't know who he was, but I can think of one reason why he said it. To get the people next door to leave."

"But why?" Then, answering her own question, "You mean, because of something that's going to happen here?"

"Isn't that possible — that someone doesn't want any witnesses, doesn't want anyone to see or hear something?"

"Yes," she whispered. "I think I figured something out while you were gone. But now . . . I'm not sure I ought to tell you about it."

"Of course you should. What is it?"

"It's about that statue that Sean talked about — the statue of Kali that Beasley had. I wondered if it might be in the house somewhere, and I started looking around and found something interesting."

She led him to a large wardrobe in the middle of one

of the parlor's long walls. There were packing cases on both sides of it, but Sara pulled one aside and pointed down. There, in the dust on the floor, were two parallel scratches.

"That wardrobe's been moved lately," said Andrew.

"That's what I thought. Do you think something — the statue, for instance — is hidden underneath it?"

"Let's move it ourselves and see."

Going to the side of the wardrobe, both of them pushed on it, and it slid to where the packing case had been. They looked down, and at first they couldn't see anything. Then Andrew went into the kitchen and got a knife, pushed the point down between two of the floorboards, and levered up. One of the boards lifted, Andrew picked it up, and there, in a hollow under the floor, was the statue Sean had told them about.

It was everything he had said it was and more: more beautiful and much, much more frightening. It was a little over two feet tall, carved out of wood, and painted so that the blood on its four hands and its open mouth was unmistakable. The necklace of skulls was bone-white, and the robe that covered the graceful, dancing body was a dusty gray. Andrew had a feeling that it was quite old. But old or not, there was no question about the effect it had on them, for they were both shaken by it.

"Well," said Andrew, his voice a little uncertain, "I know what Sean was talking about when he said it gave him the jimjams."

Sara nodded. "I wish I hadn't thought of looking for it. That I'd never seen it."

"Well, there's no harm done. We'll put it away and forget about it."

"I don't think I'll ever forget about it. I'm sure I'm going to dream about it, and—" she clutched Andrew's arm. "What's that?"

At first he did not know what she was talking about. Then he heard it too: a faint, musical chiming like the tinkling of tiny bells and, with it and over it, a kind of humming chant.

"Does it have something to do with this — the statue?" whispered Sara.

"I don't know."

They had not picked the statue up, but merely looked at it as it lay there in its hiding place under the floor. Now, working quickly, Andrew dropped the board down over it, covering it, and together they moved the wardrobe back so that it concealed the place where the statue was hidden. But the faint chiming continued, and so did the chanting, and as they stepped back, away from the wardrobe, they heard something else: a faint cry and the sound of movement upstairs.

"That's Beasley!" said Andrew.

They hurried out of the parlor, up the stairs, and into Beasley's bedroom. The first thing they saw when they burst into the room was that their old friend was no longer in bed, but crouched in the farthest corner of the room, his eyes dilated and glazed with fear. The next thing they saw was what had frightened him so, and — as was the case with the statue — they could understand the reason for his fear. For something very odd was taking place out in the foggy garden: strange shapes, glowing with an eerie blue light, were moving, apparently dancing, out there. It was they who were chanting, accompanying their movements with the silvery ringing of tiny temple bells.

"No," whispered Beasley, huddled in the corner of the room in his long nightgown. "No, no!" And Sara and Andrew both knew that this was what he had been afraid of all along.

"Who are they?" asked Sara. "What do they want?"

As if in answer, the chanting broke off and a sibilant but curiously musical voice called out, drawing out the name.

"Beasley!" it said. "Bee .... eesley! You knew we were coming, and we are here. Come out to us now. Come out!"

"No!" said Beasley again. "No, no!"

"Don't let them frighten you!" said Andrew. "We won't let you go out there. And they can't come in."

"Yes," said the voice outside. "Yes, yes, yes, Beasley. You know in whose name we speak — she who must be obeyed — and you must come out to us. You must!"

Like a sleepwalker, Beasley stood up, crossed the room, opened the bedroom door, and started down the stairs.

"Beasley, wait! Come back!" called Sara. "Where are you going?"

"You know where!" said Andrew. "Downstairs and out into the garden. And we've got to stop him! Beasley, no! Wait!"

He hurried after their friend, caught up with him when he was halfway down the stairs and took hold of his nightgown; but he might as well have tried to hold back a team of oxen. Slowly and ponderously, Beasley went on down the stairs, turned at the bottom, and started toward the rear of the house and the door that led out into the garden.

Sara had now joined Andrew. Pushing past Beasley, she stood in front of him, hands upraised.

"Listen to me. Please listen to me!" she said earnestly. "You know who we are, don't you? We're Sara and Andrew, your friends, and —"

Putting out a large hand, Beasley pushed her aside and continued along the corridor and into the back pantry, where there was a door that led out into the garden.

"Andrew, what are we going to do? We can't let him go out there!" wailed Sara.

"No," he said. Now he pushed past the slowly moving Beasley. The key was in the lock of the back door. As Andrew grabbed for it, Beasley's hand went out and took it away from him. He put it in the lock and turned it, unlocking the door. In addition to the lock, there was a heavy bolt on the door. As Andrew reached for that, determined to keep it bolted no matter what Beasley did, there was a sudden loud knock on the front door.

"Who's that?" asked Sara.

"I don't know."

There was another, even louder knock.

"Hello there! Sean! Andrew! Someone! It's Dr. Reeves. Open the door and let me in!"

"Dr. Reeves!" said Sara.

"Yes," said Andrew, using both hands to keep the bolt on the back door closed. "Go let him in. And hurry!"

He fought the seemingly sleepwalking Beasley, pushing his hands away, shoving him back, while Sara flew down the hall and opened the front door. A moment later both the doctor and his coachman came running along the hall to the pantry.

"Well, what's all this?" said Reeves sharply, taking hold of Beasley. "Shouldn't be out of bed, old chap. Certainly shouldn't be down here. You're a sick man."

"We tried to stop him," said Andrew. "He wanted to go out there, into the garden. There's something out there."

"So Sara said." Reeves glanced out into the garden, but the dancing shapes and the eerie lights were gone and all was quiet. "Whoever was there seems to be gone, but we're not going to take any chances. Help me with him, Charles," he said to his coachman. "Outside with him and into the carriage. We're taking him to hospital."

"Yes, doctor," said the coachman, taking Beasley by the other arm.

"Doesn't he need a robe or blanket or something?" asked Andrew.

"Yes. Get the blanket from the bed upstairs. In the meantime, you get both your coats," he said to Sara. "After we take him to hospital, I'm going to take the two of you home."

5

Mr. Bannerji

"A Mr. O'Farrell to see you, Master Andrew," said Matson, coming into the breakfast room. It was late for Sara and Andrew to be eating breakfast — much later than usual — but after the excitement of the previous afternoon and evening, the explanation that was required when Dr. Reeves brought them home, they had gotten to bed very late.

"O'Farrell? I don't know any Mr. O'Farrell."

"I believe he is an associate of your friend, Mr. Beasley."

Matson was a more orthodox butler than Fred was a coachman. He never said more than was absolutely necessary, but what he said was always thoughtful and usually correct.

"I'll bet it's Sean!" said Sara. "Has he got red hair?"

"Yes, he has, Miss Sara."

"Then it is Sean. Please send him in, Matson."

A moment later Sean came in, a little paler than usual and walking rather stiffly and carefully.

"Sean!" said Sara, running to him and throwing her arms around him. "We've been very worried about you. Are you all right?"

"Yes and no," he said, wincing. "Please don't joggle me. If you do, I'm afraid my head might fall off."

"Why?" asked Andrew. "And what happened to you yesterday afternoon?"

"I was coshed."

"Coshed?"

"Hit on the back of the head with a cosh or a neddie or a sock full of sand."

"By whom?" asked Sara.

"I wish I knew. I was on my way to the house, just crossing the street from the builder's yard, when someone came up behind me and bashed me."

"And you don't know who it was?" asked Andrew.

"No. Couldn't see 'em because of the fog, but I suspect there was more than one of them, at least two and maybe three. When I came to, I was lying in a shed in the yard with the grandfather of all headaches. The door had been braced shut, and by the time I got it open and went over to Mr. Beasley's house, you and he were gone, but I found your note saying the doctor was taking him to hospital."

"Two or three of them," said Sara. "They were probably the same gang that gave us such a scare later on."

"What do you mean?"

They told him everything that had happened, and he whistled softly.

"I told you it had something to do with that statue," he said.

"You can't be sure of that," said Andrew.

He gave Sean a pax sign, indicating he should mind what he said as Sara's mother bustled in. For of course they had told her very little of what had happened, just enough to explain their lateness. They introduced Sean, and she said she was happy to meet him and was sorry to hear about Mr. Beasley's illness and hoped he'd be better soon. She asked Sean if he'd had breakfast, and when he said he had, she insisted that he have some tea or coffee anyway and, as a result, it was about twenty minutes before they could get away.

They had arranged for Fred to take them to the hospital. Now, of course, Sean would go with them. He asked if they could stop at the shop on their way as he had suddenly realized that he had left a good deal of money in the till and he was a little worried about it; and they said they did not mind at all.

Fred stopped in front of the shop, and Sara and Andrew got out of the landau with Sean but waited outside while he went into the shop. They were looking in the window of the shop next door — a window that was full of china and old silver — when Whispering Willie, the dustman, drew up in his cart.

"Wotcher, mate," said Fred. "Am I in your way?"

"Ta, but nix, cully," wheezed Willie. "I ain't collecting here today. I just stopped by to see if there was any word on me old chum, Beasley."

"We're not sure," said Sara. "We're on our way to see him now at St. Mary's."

"The 'orspital?"

"That's right."

"When'd he go there?"

"Last night."

"Does that mean he's worse'n what he was?"

"Not necessarily," said Andrew. "It just means the doctor wanted him there."

"I 'opes he knows what he's doing — the doc, I mean. I don't 'old with 'orspitals meself. You sometimes gets sicker there than you was when you come in. But will you tell him what I told you yesterday — that old Whispering Willie was asking for him?"

"We certainly will."

"Ta, then." He turned to go back to his cart and bumped into a dark, heavyset gentleman who was coming up the street. "Oops-a-daisy! Sorry, guv'ner."

"You should be sorry!" said the man, flushing angrily. "You dirty, smelly lout!"

"Who're you calling a dirty louse?" said Willie just as angrily.

"Never mind," said the man, drawing back as if the very sight of the dustman was offensive. "Please." And he stood aside to let Willie climb up on to his cart.

"Bloomin' toff!" muttered Willie. "Our own is bad enough. But furrin ones. . . ." He spat, shook the reins, and sent the shaggy, slow-moving horse on up the street.

Sean had come out of the shop and joined Sara and Andrew. The three of them were looking at the dark gentleman, and he in turn was looking at them. He was wearing a loosely fitting, sober suit of foreign cut with a cape over it. He carried a whangee-handled umbrella and his hat was black, broad-brimmed, and flat-crowned.

"Excuse me," the man said to Sean. "You are an associate of Mr. Beasley?"

"Yes, I am."

"Allow me to introduce myself," he said in correct but somewhat stilted English. "My name is Bannerji. Gopal Bannerji, formerly of Benares University, presently with the East India Company." He took out a card case, extracted a card from it, and presented it with a bow to Sean.

Sean read it, then introduced himself. "Sean O'Farrell. And this is Miss Sara Wiggins and Mr. Andrew Tillett, both old friends of Mr. Beasley."

"There is nothing nicer than old friends," said Mr. Bannerji, smiling. "Especially when they are so young. Before we go any further, may I apologize to you?"

"For what?" asked Sean.

"My momentary lapse in behavior toward that dustman. Miss Wiggins and Mr. Tillett both frowned during my exchange with him, and I felt I should explain.

I am, of course, an Indian. As you probably know, we have a caste system in which the Brahmans are the highest caste and the Untouchables are the lowest. I am a Brahman, and a dustman is an Untouchable. If an Untouchable even comes close to me, I am thought to be defiled. Of course, you here in England have no such beliefs. Did not the Scottish poet, Robert Burns, write a poem that states that a man's a man for all that? However, the habits of a lifetime are strong. And so, when I was brought into sudden and unexpected contact with the dustman, I reacted as I did. Will you forgive me?"

"I suppose so," said Sean. "Were you looking for Mr. Beasley?"

"I was. A most intelligent man. I've had several interesting chats with him. Is he here?"

"No, he's not. He's been sick for several days, and he's now in St. Mary's Hospital."

"Oh, I'm sorry to hear that — very sorry. What's wrong with him?"

"Well, Beasley himself kept saying it was influenza or some kind of fever, but the doctor wasn't sure about that. We're just going over there to see what the word is."

"Oh, may I come with you? I am not, of course, an associate of his as you are or an old friend as the two young people here are. But as I said I admire him, and I am concerned about him."

Sean glanced at Sara and Andrew.

"Why, yes," said Andrew. "I can't guarantee that

you'll be able to see him. I'm not sure that we'll be able to ourselves. But you're welcome to come with us."

"Thank you," said Bannerji. "Thank you very much."

He helped Sara into the carriage, insisted on getting in last himself, and chatted pleasantly all the way to the hospital about how much he liked London and about his work at the East India Company. When they got to the hospital, he made a point of hanging back while Andrew inquired at the admission desk and then led the way upstairs to the ward where they had seen Dr. Reeves the day before. The sister on duty remembered Andrew and Sara, told them to wait, and a few minutes later Dr. Reeves came out. He greeted Sara, Andrew, and Sean and bowed to Mr. Bannerji when he was introduced.

"It's hard to say how he is," he said when they asked about Beasley. "On the whole he's better — quite a bit better — but he's not completely well yet by any means, and I'm still not sure what's wrong with him."

"You've no idea at all?" asked Andrew.

"I didn't say that. I said I wasn't sure." He looked at Andrew for a moment, then at Sara and Sean. "I'd like to try something. He doesn't know me, but he does know the three of you. Come on into the room with me."

"He knows me, also," said Mr. Bannerji. "Not well, but slightly. May I come, too?"

"Yes, of course," said Dr. Reeves.

He led the way down the corridor, opened a door, and ushered them into a small, typical hospital room.

Beasley, looking better than he had the day before — and far less anxious — was sitting propped up in bed.

"Well, here's a sight worth seeing," said Sean, pretending to be casual but unable to hide either his affection for Beasley or his concern.

"Oh, hello, Sean," said Beasley in a flat, rather weak voice. "Hello, Sara, Andrew."

"Then you know these people," said Dr. Reeves.

"Of course I know them," said Beasley testily. "Why shouldn't I know them?"

"There were times yesterday when you didn't know anything."

"And do you remember me also, Mr. Beasley?" asked Bannerji.

"Yes, I think so," said Beasley, studying him. "You're the Indian who talked to me about the statue of Kali that I had in the window."

"Kali or Bhowani, yes. When I was there this morning, I noticed it was no longer there."

"No, I got rid of it."

"How?"

"I'd rather not say."

"Perhaps that is best."

"I'd like to ask you about something else," said Dr. Reeves. "I'd like you to tell me what happened yesterday."

"You asked me that before," said Beasley. "And I told you I don't remember."

"You don't remember anything at all about it?"

"No."

"When did you first start feeling ill?"

"Oh, about a week ago."

"Can you tell me anything significant that happened between that time and yesterday?"

"I don't know what you mean by significant."

"Well, Mr. O'Farrell and your two young friends, Sara and Andrew, all claimed that during most of yesterday you seemed very anxious, afraid of something."

"I don't know why I should have been. If I was, I don't remember why."

"I see." Dr. Reeves looked at him thoughtfully, then turned to Sara and Andrew. "Would one of you tell Mr. Beasley what you told me last night — about his state generally, and especially what happened just before I arrived."

They did it together, Sara starting and Andrew finishing, recalling Beasley's very evident fear, then his irrationality, and finally describing, as well as they could, the strange happenings in the garden: the eerie lights, the voices calling, and Beasley's attempt to go out there.

Beasley fidgeted through the recital, arranging the pillows behind his head, pushing his blanket away, but Andrew had the feeling that he was listening intently to everything that was said.

"I'm sorry," he said. "I don't remember any of that."

"You don't remember any part of it?"

"No. And I'm getting very tired and sleepy. Would you mind if I took a nap?"

"No, Mr. Beasley. I think that's a good idea."

They said good-bye and left. Dr. Reeves led them up the corridor until they were out of earshot of the room.

"Well?" he said. "What do you think?"

"He seems much better," said Sean. "Much more his old self and much less anxious."

"I thought so, too," said Sara. "I also think he remembered more of what happened than he let on."

"I agree," said Andrew. "Now will you tell us what's wrong with him? I gather you don't think its influenza or anything like that."

"No," said Dr. Reeves. "I think he was drugged."

"Why?" said Sara. "How and by whom?"

"I certainly don't know why or by whom. And it would take a good deal of investigating to determine how it was administered. But I suspect he's been given some kind of drug that induces hallucinations."

"Well, whatever it was," said Sean, "I'll bet it had something to do with that heathen statue!"

"Would you care to comment on any of this, Mr. Bannerji?" said Dr. Reeves.

"If you would not consider it presumptuous, there are a few things I might say. The statue, as you must have gathered, was that of Kali, also known as Bhowani, the consort of Shiva and a very revered and powerful goddess. Now one of the things that puzzled and worried me from the beginning — that is, from the moment I first saw it in Mr. Beasley's shop window — was that he would not say where he had gotten it, just as he would not tell us now what he had done with it."

"Was it valuable?" asked Dr. Reeves.

"Yes and no. It is not like these ridiculous and romantic tales one has read where the idol has an eye that is a fabulous diamond or ruby. But the statue was fairly old — I should say sixteenth century — and authentic. I told this to Mr. Beasley, and I also told him I did not think it was wise to keep it in his window where a devotee of Kali might be tempted to steal it. I think, from the young people's description of what happened last night, that something like that might have been going on there."

"That's one of the things that occurred to me," said Sean.

"As to drugs, we have almost as many as we have religious sects. I am not just talking about opium, which is very common. I am talking about bhang, which is also known as hashish, and which, as I'm sure you know, can cause either pleasurable or terrifying hallucinations."

"Yes, I know about opium and hashish and their effects, but I don't believe Mr. Beasley was given either of those. I think he was given something else — something I have not been able to identify yet."

"That may well be. However, he is better?"

"Yes. He's considerably better."

"That brings me to the point I wanted to make. To a

suggestion that I hope you and his friends here will consider. Without knowing all the facts, we seem to be in general agreement that compatriots of mine — that is to say, Indians — might well be behind what has happened to Mr. Beasley. Is this true?" He glanced around at them, and they all nodded. "If this is so — if they want something from Mr. Beasley that they still have not gotten — isn't it possible that he is still in danger?"

"You mean, even here in hospital?" said Sara.

"Don't you think that is possible?"

"I suppose it would be if they knew where he was," said Sean. "But how would they know that?"

"From what you have said, it's clear that they were keeping a close watch on Mr. Beasley's house. Don't you think they would have followed Dr. Reeves' carriage when he brought him here?"

"Yes, they could very well have done that," said Dr. Reeves. "And while I think that, on the whole, he is quite safe here, I would like to know what you're leading up to — what you're suggesting."

"I grant you that he is fairly safe here," said Bannerji. "But wouldn't he be even safer if he was moved to a place that our Indian friends didn't know about?"

"Where, for instance?" asked Dr. Reeves.

"I don't know. A nursing home to which he would be transported at night so that no one would know he was being moved. Or even a private home if the right one could be found."

"What about our place?" asked Andrew.

"Yours?" said Dr. Reeves.

"Yes. It's in St. John's Wood, which is very respectable and well protected. We have a large house, so we have plenty of room. And we also have quite a few people there to help take care of him."

"It's an idea," said Sean. "If you don't mind, it has many advantages."

"I not only don't mind, I'd like it very much," said Andrew. "And I'm sure that my mother and Sara's mother and Peter Wyatt would approve, too."

"Well, I have no objections," said Dr. Reeves. "In fact, I can see some advantages to it, too. But I think that if we're going to do it, we should do it in the manner that Mr. Bannerji suggested — quietly and secretly, at night."

"Can that be arranged?" asked Bannerji.

"It can. We'll bundle him up, and I'll take him there myself in my own carriage when I leave here tonight."

6

The Secret Name

Beasley's move to the house in St. John's Wood took place that night in exactly the way that Dr. Reeves had suggested. Mrs. Wiggins had not only approved of the idea, but was enthusiastic about it. There had been little enough for her to do with Andrew's mother away, and there were few things she liked better than being able to nurse someone and fuss over them. Though she had not met Beasley before, she had of course heard a good deal about him from Sara and Andrew, and you would never have known that they weren't old friends from the reception she gave him when Dr. Reeves brought him to the house at about ten o'clock that night. A bed in one of the guest rooms had been made ready for him. Mrs. Wiggins stood by while Dr. Reeves and his coachman helped Beasley up the stairs and got him into bed. Then she took over, listened gravely to Dr. Reeves' instructions and, shooing everyone else out, remained with Beasley until he fell asleep.

Sean came to the house just as Sara and Andrew were finishing breakfast the next morning. Mrs. Wiggins reported that their patient had had a very good night, was feeling much better, and would be delighted to see all of them. They went up and found that her report had been accurate. Beasley not only looked better, he insisted that he felt that way, said he was going to ask Dr. Reeves if he couldn't get up that afternoon. When Sean suggested that he shouldn't rush his fences that way, he pretended to get angry, said that Sean had been loafing and ordered him to go back to the shop where he might — just possibly — be able to earn what he was being paid. Sean told him that he was an ungrateful hypochondriac, said he'd be glad to go back to the shop — glad to do anything that would get him away from Beasley's bad temper and left. He winked, however, at Sara and Andrew as he did so and told them under his breath that he'd be back that afternoon.

Dr. Reeves came to the house at about noon and was very pleased with Beasley's progress. In addition to the medicine that Beasley had been taking at the hospital, which he had brought with him, Dr. Reeves now gave him a sleeping draught and left instructions on when and how it was to be taken. Just as he was leaving, Mr. Bannerji arrived and was as delighted as everyone at Beasley's progress.

"Then this comes at an auspicious time," he said, giving Beasley a small package. "In fact, it may even speed your recovery."

"What is it?" asked Beasley.

"Open it and see."

Beasley tore off the paper, revealing a small painting in a simple black frame.

"It's Mogul, isn't it?" said Beasley.

"Yes, late 18th century, near the end of the Mogul dynasty. Considering the uncertain nature of your illness, I feared to bring you any food — even a sweet. And I was not sure that flowers would be appropriate. But no one could object to flowers of this sort."

The painting, stylized and brightly colored, was of an Indian garden with a fountain playing in the midst of ornate flower beds.

"It's very nice indeed," said Beasley. "Thank you very much."

"Careful," said Sean, as Bannerji backed into the small night table.

"Sorry," said Bannerji, catching the table as it rocked and the bottles on it clinked together. "I am, I fear, a rather clumsy man. You really do like it?" he said to Beasley. "If you do not care for the subject and would prefer something else — a portrait, perhaps. . . ."

"No," said Beasley. "It's very thoughtful of you, and I like it very much, prefer it by far to real flowers."

He gave it to Sean, who put it on the bureau, and they all looked at it appreciatively.

It was about this time that Matson made his contribution to the comfort of the house's guest and patient, suggesting that he might like to have a barber come in and shave him. Feeling the grizzled stubble on his face, Beasley said that he would, and Matson said he would arrange to have one there in the morning.

By late afternoon, a change had come over Beasley. He seemed listless, uncomfortable, and his eyes not only lost their sparkle, but began to look troubled and anxious. He seemed withdrawn, snapped at Sean when he came to see him at about six o'clock and, to Mrs. Wiggins' distress, ate very little of his supper.

Sean stayed for supper, and they had a conference afterward. Mrs. Wiggins attended as well as Sean, Sara, and Andrew. They decided that though Beasley was clearly not as well as he had been in the morning, the change was not serious enough to warrant calling Dr. Reeves. Mrs. Wiggins gave Beasley the sleeping draught that Dr. Reeves had left, and he fell asleep almost immediately and slept fitfully through most of the night.

Andrew, however, did not sleep particularly well. He woke up three or four times without knowing why, and each time went into Beasley's room. The last time, at about two in the morning, he found Sara there. They listened to Beasley's heavy breathing. Sara pulled the blanket up to cover him, then they went outside.

"Why aren't you asleep?" asked Andrew.

"Why aren't you?"

"I was, but I woke up."

"So did I." She looked at him thoughtfully. "Andrew, I'm worried."

"I don't think there's anything to be worried about. He's not that much worse than he was."

"I'm not sure about that. But that's not the only thing I'm worried about. I have a feeling something's going on outside, something bad."

"What do you mean?"

"I looked out the window when I woke up a little while ago, and I thought I saw someone or something out in the garden."

Andrew knew her too well to scoff at the idea.

"Show me where."

They went into her room without putting on the light and stood near the window; there she pointed to the dark mass of shrubbery near the kitchen. He studied it carefully.

"There doesn't seem to be anyone there now. You couldn't tell who it was?"

"No. Except . . . well, he seemed to be wearing a long robe and a turban."

"In other words, an Indian."

"Yes. I admit I don't know how anyone could know that Beasley is here. The whole point of moving him from hospital at night was so that nobody *would* know, but. . . ." She paused, frowning. "You kept looking back when we were on our way here, and when I asked you what you were looking at, you said nothing. Were you telling the truth?"

"I don't know. When we first left the hospital, I thought a four-wheeler was following us. But by the time we got to Marylebone Road it was gone."

"By that time whoever it was may have guessed where we were going." Then, as he started for the door, "Wait a minute. You're not going out there, out into the garden, are you?"

"Well, if you're worried because you think someone's out there. . . ."

"I'd be much more worried if you went out to see! Will you promise me that you won't go out?"

He hesitated, then said, "All right. I think it was probably just your imagination. We're all a bit nervy. We'll see in the morning."

And in the morning they did see. They were just finishing breakfast when Matson came in carrying Andrew's mother's trug, the flat basket she used when she was gardening. On the surface he was as imperturbable as a good butler always is, but by now Andrew had learned to read shadings in his expression.

"Good morning, Matson," he said. "Anything wrong?"

"Not necessarily wrong, Master Andrew, but something rather curious. When I unlocked the door this morning, I found this hanging over the knob." He took some flowers out of the basket, a string of red poppies whose stems had been braided together to make a long chain. "There was another one, just like it, over the knob of the kitchen door."

Sara sat up straighter, and she paled.

"That is strange," said Andrew. "There was no note with them?"

"No, Master Andrew."

"I wonder how they got there."

"They were undoubtedly put there sometime during the night."

"Yes. Well, I don't think it's anything to worry about."

"No, Mr. Andrew. Do you wish to examine them or shall I remove them."

"You can get rid of them, Matson."

"Yes, Master Andrew."

"Well," said Andrew as Matson took the flowers out, "you were right; there must have been someone outside the house last night. But I still don't think it's anything to worry about."

"You don't? What was the purpose of bringing him here rather than letting him stay in hospital?"

"To protect him."

"Right. That's why Dr. Reeves brought him here at night. So that no one would know where he was. But the flowers prove that, whoever the men are who are after him, they know where he is."

"It may not be the same people," he said unconvincingly.

"No? Who did leave them, then?"

"I don't know."

He didn't want to say so, but he knew that she was right. He also knew that she was probably thinking the same thing he was: that the string of scarlet poppies hanging over the knob must have made the door look as if it had been splashed with blood.

They finished their breakfast in silence and were just leaving the table when the barber Matson had ordered arrived. Andrew went upstairs with him to Beasley's room. Mrs. Wiggins had said that Beasley was up but didn't want any breakfast yet. That was all she said, and perhaps she wasn't aware of it, but Andrew saw at once that their friend was not at all well; that he was, in fact, worse than yesterday.

The barber had brought a gladstone bag in which he carried the various things he was going to need: a large brass basin, a smaller crescent-shaped one that he held under the chin of the man he was shaving to catch the lather, his razors, strop, brush, and soap. Annie, the upstairs maid, came in with a pitcher of hot water and, tucking a towel around Beasley's neck, the barber set to work.

Either the barber was a naturally silent man or he was

used to shaving invalids who preferred silence to talk, for — after saying good morning to Beasley — he said nothing more until he was finished and drying Beasley's face. Then he spoke to Andrew rather than Beasley and asked whether he'd like him to come again the next morning. When Andrew said he would, he said that in that case — if Andrew did not object — he would leave his bag and the things that were in it so he would not have to bring them in the morning. Andrew said he didn't object and, bowing to him and Beasley, the barber left.

There was no need for Andrew to ask his friend how he was. Besides his pallor, the dew of perspiration on his forehead and upper lip, his eyes told the story: they were not merely dull and lackluster, they were haunted again, filled with anxiety that was almost as acute as the terror Andrew and Sara had found in them the afternoon before they had taken him to the hospital.

There was a perfunctory knock, and Dr. Reeves came in. He nodded to Andrew, then, looking at Beasley, frowned. Taking out his stethoscope, he told Andrew to wait outside while he examined his patient. Sara and Mrs. Wiggins had come upstairs with him, and they were waiting in the hall outside the door.

"He's not doing well at all, is he, the poor man?" said Mrs. Wiggins when Andrew joined them.

"I'm afraid not," said Andrew.

"I can't understand it," said Mrs. Wiggins. "He seemed

much better yesterday morning. Then, all of a sudden, he's worse."

Dr. Reeves came out of the room about ten minutes later.

"He's bad again, isn't he, doctor?" said Mrs. Wiggins.

"Yes, he is," said Reeves. He paused as Matson came up the stairs with a note on a silver salver. "Is that for me?"

"No, doctor. For Mr. Beasley," said Matson. He tapped on the door and went in. Andrew wondered who the note was from, but Sara was only interested in what they had been discussing.

"Have you any idea why this happened?" she asked.

"No, I haven't. I told you the other day that I didn't think it was influenza or any similar disease. That he might have been given some kind of drug. Well, I still think that, though I haven't identified the drug as yet and I've no idea how more could have been given to him. On the other hand, he could merely be reacting to the original dose."

"Does that happen?" asked Andrew.

"It can, just as a patient with a high fever can have a remission and be normal for a day or so and then have the fever again."

"And what shall we do in the meantime, doctor?" asked Mrs. Wiggins. "Do you have any special instructions for us?"

"No. I would go light on his food, but give him plenty of liquids and continue with the medication I left for him. I'll try to see him again this evening. If I can't, I'll be here tomorrow morning. And if he's no better, I'll want him back in hospital."

He left, and Mrs. Wiggins told Sara and Andrew to go out for a walk or do something and she'd go in and stay with Beasley. Sara and Andrew went downstairs, but they did not go out for a walk; and when Mrs. Wiggins came down about an hour later, she said she had been able to get Mr. Beasley to take some beef tea and he was now asleep. Andrew was a little dubious about this. He had noticed that when their friend did not want to talk, he closed his eyes and pretended to be napping.

About four-thirty, Sean arrived. He was explaining that he was too worried about Beasley to stay in the shop when Bannerji was shown in. They both wanted to know how Beasley was, and Sara and Andrew told them about his worsening condition and what Dr. Reeves had said about it. Frowning, Bannerji asked if anything unsual had happened during the night, and Andrew told him about the flowers on the door knobs. Reacting to Bannerji's frown, Sean asked if the flowers were significant.

"Yes, they were," said Bannerji. "We are all worried about our friend, and I assure you that we have reason to be."

"Why?" asked Sean. "Do you know what's behind everything that's going on?"

"I have some idea of what it's about," said Bannerji. "Would it be possible to see Mr. Beasley? If it is, I'd like to talk to him."

"Let's see," said Sara.

She led the way upstairs, looked into Beasley's room and, finding him awake, talked to him for a moment and then ushered the others in. Sean and Bannerji both greeted him, and it was clear that they were both shocked by his appearance.

"Mr. Beasley, sir," said Bannerji, "I do not know if you are prepared to think of me as a friend. I have not known you for as long — nor of course do I know you as well — as Mr. O'Farrell and the two young people here. Nevertheless, I hope you are assured of my good will. That being so, I think the time has come to speak frankly. Dr. Reeves has said that he does not believe that your condition is the result of illness or natural causes. That has been my feeling from the beginning."

"What do you think is wrong with him, then?" asked Sean.

"It may be that he has been given drugs of some sort as Dr. Reeves suggested. But, on the other hand, he may have been exposed to strong mental influences about which you in the West know very little."

"You mean a spell, something like that?" asked Andrew.

"You can call it that if you like. As you know, we in the East have several disciplines — like yoga — that have been practiced for centuries with very interesting results.

In any case, much as I deplore it, I believe that Mr. Beasley has angered some of my countrymen and they are responsible for what is happening to him. Does that sound logical to you, Mr. Beasley?"

Sitting up in bed, his face pale and waxy, Beasley nodded.

"Does it have anything to do with that statue of Kali?"

"I don't think so," Beasley said hoarsely.

"Does it have something to do with something else? Something we don't know about?"

"I don't know."

"You mean you have no idea why they have been persecuting you? Whether it's revenge they want or something else?"

"No."

"That's strange. If it's something they want, I would have expected them to communicate with you. On the other hand, they may think you know what they want. And, in fact, you may without being aware of it."

"I don't," said Beasley, shaking his head.

"Are you interested in finding out whether you do or don't?"

"How?"

"I talked before about yoga, about which, I regret to say, I know very little. On the other hand, I know a good deal about a western discipline that is not unlike it. I studied in Paris under a disciple of Dr. Janet."

"You're talking about hypnotism?" said Andrew.

"Yes. As you probably know, under hypnosis, one can remember things that one cannot remember in a waking state. What do you say, Mr. Beasley? Would you consider letting me hypnotize you?"

Andrew looked at Beasley. His feelings about Bannerji's suggestion were strangely mixed. He had never seen anyone hypnotized and was very interested in how it was done. At the same time, there was something about Bannerji's doing it that he found worrying. And apparently he wasn't alone in feeling that way.

"I don't know," said Beasley.

"Does the thought of it make you anxious?"

"A little."

"It does most people. But I assure you that there is no danger, nothing to fear. Not only that, but your friends here will be watching to make sure that no harm comes to you."

"They can all stay?"

"They not only can, I insist that they do. I can only hypnotize you if you trust me, and I suspect you will only be willing to trust me if you feel you are safe, protected."

"You're right," said Beasley. He looked at Sara, Andrew, and Sean, then back at Bannerji. "All right. You can hypnotize me."

"Good," said Bannerji. "First of all, I'd like to darken the room a little." He drew all the curtains, then lit the gas jet over Beasley's bed. "Second, I'd like the three of you to move back a little so the sight of you will not distract Mr. Beasley."

Andrew moved back until he was standing in the corner behind the table on which the barber had left his gear, and Sara and Sean did the same.

"Now," said Bannerji, seating himself near the foot of Beasley's bed, "I want you to get comfortable, as comfortable as you can make yourself." He waited while Beasley slid down a little and adjusted the pillow under his head. "Are you comfortable now?"

"Yes," whispered Beasley.

"Splendid," said Bannerji. He took out his albert, the chain to which his gold watch was attached. A flat, round crystal, something like a lens, was fastened to the other end of the chain. "As I said before, faith — confidence — is necessary if the hypnosis is to be successful. You must be willing to submit your will to mine. Are you willing to do that?"

Beasley nodded.

"Very good," said Bannerji. He held up the crystal and began to spin it, turning it to the right, then to the left, then back to the right again. And as it turned, it flashed in the gaslight. "Relax. Relax completely, emptying your mind of all thought, all feeling, and look at this spinning crystal. Concentrate on it. That's it. It's going to make you sleepy; I can see your eyes becoming heavy already and wanting to close; that is good because you are tired, sleepy, and of course you have nothing to fear because your friends are here, watching over you." Bannerji continued talking in a quiet, reassuring voice; and watching the crystal spinning, first one way and then the other, focusing the light of the gas jet and then breaking it up, Andrew felt himself getting sleepy.

"You are now in the first stage of hypnosis," said Bannerji. "A stage in which you can hear me perfectly but no longer have any control over your body. For instance, although you can move your left hand, you cannot move your right. Isn't that so? Try to move your right hand."

Beasley strained — Andrew could see him trying to move his right hand — but it remained motionless on the bed.

"Very good," said Bannerji. "We are now ready to begin. Is it true that you are in danger, threatened by someone?"

"Yes," whispered Beasley.

"Do you know who it is that is threatening you?"

"Yes."

"Is it, as I have suggested, a group of my compatriots — in other words, Indians?"

"Yes."

"Do you know why they are a danger to you, threatening you?"

"Yes."

"Is it because of something that you have and they want: that statue of Kali, for instance?"

"No."

"Is it because of something you have done, then?"

"No. At least . . . not in the way you mean."

"Is it, then, because of something you know? A piece of information?"

"Yes," said Beasley. He was breathing a little faster now, speaking with more difficulty.

"Is it perhaps a place? A place where something is hidden?"

"No."

"Is it a name, then? A name that you know and the men about whom we have been talking want you to tell them?"

"Yes." Sweat had broken out on Beasley's forehead and upper lip. His left hand was clenching and unclenching, and even the right one — the one he could not move — was twitching.

"What is the name?"

"It's . . ." He swallowed. "I can't tell you."

"You must tell me!"

"I can't! I promised I never would! I—" He broke off, clearly in the grip of some powerful emotion.

"I repeat, you must tell me the name!"

"I tell you, I can't! I . . . I . . ."

Something happened to Andrew. Half hypnotized himself, fascinated by what was taking place, nevertheless he suddenly could not let the process go on, could not let Beasley continue to be subjected to pressure that was making him writhe as if he were in physical pain. With a sudden movement, he pushed first the large brass basin and then the small one off the table. They fell to the floor, one after the other, rattling and ringing, filling the small room with their metallic clangor.

Beasley stiffened and sat up as if cold water had been dashed in his face. Then, as Bannerji turned with an exclamation and glared at Andrew, Beasley said, "What is this? What are you all doing in here?"

"Mr. Bannerji hypnotized you," said Sara. "Don't you remember?"

"No. Why did he do that?"

"To get to the bottom of what's been happening to you," said Sean. "To try to find out who the Indians that have been after you are and what they want."

"It's none of his business! Or yours either! Now get out of here — all of you!"

"May I remind you of who we are, Mr. Beasley?" said Bannerji. "We are your friends — all of us — and concerned about you."

"I don't care who you are! I want you all out of here!"

Sean looked at the others, then stood up.

"All right, Mr. Beasley. Just as you say." He led the way out. "I'm sorry," he said to Mr. Bannerji.

"Please," said Bannerji, raising a forgiving hand. "One does the best one can. With your approval, I tried to help. If it was to no avail, it was not my fault, for we were close — very close — to the answer. As for his hostility toward me, that is very common in a posthypnotic state."

"Well, it was too bad!" said Sara. "I'm sure he'll be sorry about it when he's better."

"I'm sure he will, too. But, in the meantime, I will go. May I come back to see how he is tomorrow?"

"Of course," said Sara.

Bowing to them, Bannerji left and, turning, Sean looked at Andrew.

"You're very quiet," he said. "What's wrong?"

"Nothing."

"Something *is* wrong," said Sara. "Are you upset because you knocked over those basins?"

"No."

"No?" She looked at him curiously. "I wondered if you'd done it on purpose. Did you?"

"Yes."

"Why?"

"I didn't like what was going on."

"I know," said Sean. "It was rough on old Beasley, but Bannerji was trying to help." He paused. "Or don't you think so?"

"I don't know," said Andrew irritably. "I didn't like what was going on then, and I don't like what's going on now. The truth is, I'm worried!"

"We all are, Andrew," said Sara reasonably. "But the truth also is that we don't know what to be worried *about*."

"I know that, too. What do you think is making me so shirty? I've got a feeling that things are coming to a head.

7 0

That's why . . . well, I don't think we should leave Beasley alone tonight."

Sara didn't argue with Andrew. She had learned to respect his instincts as he respected hers. But surprisingly, Sean seemed willing to accept what he said, too.

"We could do it easily if the three of us took turns watching him," he said. "I don't think we should worry your mother," he told Sara, "but why don't you invite me to stay for supper so I can see what Dr. Reeves says when he comes back? And, after that, you can suggest that since it's so late, I should stay overnight. Then we can make our own arrangements about who stays with him when."

"And if Dr. Reeves doesn't come back?" asked Andrew.

"We won't be sure about that until about nine or ten o'clock, which will be late enough so that there'll be all the more reason for me to stay."

"Will you stay for supper, Sean?" Sara asked with no change of expression. "We're having one of Mrs. Simmons' specialties, Wiltshire gammon with Cumberland sauce, which I happen to know you like."

"I love any kind of ham, Sara," said Sean, his face as expressionless as hers, "but I love Wiltshire gammon best of all. Thank you very much."

7

The Vigil and After

As often happens when you've made careful plans, things worked out even better than the three expected. Mrs. Wiggins herself invited Sean to stay for supper, was delighted at his enthusiasm for the ham and, when Dr. Reeves had not come back to look at Beasley again by nine-thirty, suggested that he stay overnight instead of going home.

She settled him in the second guest room, went in to look at Beasley and give him the medicine Dr. Reeves had left for him, then went to bed herself. They had arranged that Sara would take the first watch, Andrew the second, and Sean the last. Andrew heard Sara slip into Beasley's room shortly after her mother had left; then he fell asleep and did not wake again until Sara shook him a little after midnight.

"How is he?" he whispered.

"He seems all right. He was asleep when I went in, and he's still asleep."

"Nothing else happened?"

"No."

"Good." He put on his robe and slippers. "See you in the morning."

Beasley was still asleep when Andrew went into the room and sat down in the big armchair near the window, but he seemed to be sleeping more quietly, breathing more easily, than he had earlier in the day.

The room was fairly dark, the only light the glow of the gaslight out in the street, and for a moment Andrew wondered if he dared bring in a candle so he could read. But he decided he'd better not. It was important that Beasley sleep, and any additional light in the room might wake him. However, he'd have to be careful that *he* didn't fall asleep, or the whole purpose of their vigil would be defeated.

He sat there in the faint breeze that came in through the open window, peering through the half darkness at the figure in the bed and listening to his breathing. And, as he had when he and Sara had been at Beasley's house, he thought about the change that had come over their old friend. He could not help but believe that if old Beasley was afraid — Beasley who had been equal to any situation, no matter how difficult — then there must be good reason for it.

He didn't know when he fell asleep. He wasn't even

conscious of feeling sleepy; but suddenly, sitting up with a start, he knew that he had been asleep and that Beasley, now sitting up in bed, was awake.

"Hello," he said.

"Hello. It's Andrew, isn't it?"

"Yes."

"What are you doing here?"

"Keeping an eye on you. You've been sick, you know."

"Yes, I know. Was Sara in here before?"

"Yes. And Sean's coming in later. He'll be with you until morning."

"Why? Are you afraid something may happen to me?"

"Something like that. Some pretty strange things have been going on."

"Yes, they have, strange as a whistling pig, they've been."

"Do you know what's behind it? What it's all about?"

"Maybe I do and maybe I don't. But if I do, it's better if you don't. In fact, the less you know, the better."

"All right."

"When's the inspector coming back?"

"The day after tomorrow."

"Is that definite?"

"As definite as these things can be. On the one hand, he's coming back from the continent and there are railroad schedules and channel steamers to be concerned about. On the other hand, he's due at the Yard, and I'm sure he won't want to be late there."

"No. You want to know something? You're all right, Andrew. You and Sara and Sean. You're all all right, have been all through these last few days, and I won't forget it."

"Oh, sure." He put on his best Cockney accent. "We'ave been blooming wonders, we have. Three right ream and rorty coves."

"Well, you have been — in spite of that shoful accent that you shouldn't even try."

"All right, I won't. Now can I give you or get you anything?"

"No. I'm going back to sleep. See you in the morning."

He was soon snoring quietly, and he continued to sleep soundly for the rest of Andrew's watch. When the grandfather clock out in the hall struck three, Andrew went in to wake Sean and, though he himself had awakened almost immediately when Sara shook him, he didn't have such an easy time of it with Sean. In fact, he had such a difficult time, shaking him and telling him to wake up, that Sara came into the room to see what the trouble was.

"Are you going to be all right?" asked Andrew, looking at Sean, who was sitting up in bed and groaning softly. "Will you be able to stay up until morning?"

"I think so," said Sean. "I've had a couple of bad nights, but I'll be fine. The thing is, do you think I might have a cup of good, strong tea to keep me awake?"

"I'll make it," said Andrew.

"I'll come down with you," said Sara. "The stove's

probably out, and I can get it going again more quickly than you."

Sean went into Beasley's room, and Sara and Andrew went downstairs, through the dining room and pantry into the kitchen. Sara was right. The stove was almost out, but she put in some more coal and opened the damper before she put the kettle on. Andrew, meanwhile, went scouting in the pantry and found the remains of the Banbury cake they had had for tea. He cut a slice for Sara, a slice for himself, and a good-sized wedge for Sean. He took it into the kitchen, and he and Sara ate their portions while they waited for the kettle to boil. When the tea had steeped, they took the steaming cup and the thick wedge of cake upstairs to Sean. His face lit up when he saw the cake as well as the tea. He thanked them, said he was sure he'd be able to stay awake after such provender, and promised to wake them early the next morning.

But it wasn't Sean who woke Andrew. It was Sara.

"What is it?" he asked, sitting up in bed. "What's wrong?"

"Put on your robe, and I'll show you," she said, her face grave.

Putting on his robe and slippers, he glanced at his watch. It was almost eight o'clock. Why hadn't Sean awakened him? He followed Sara into Beasley's room. She opened the door and stood back. He started to go in, then paused, staring. Sean was sprawled in the armchair near the window still fast asleep — in fact snoring — and the bed was empty. Beasley was gone.

"Where's Beasley?" asked Andrew.

"I don't know. He was gone when I came in here. And Sean was asleep, just as he is now."

"Maybe he knows." He went over and shook him. "Sean, wake up! Do you hear me? Wake up!"

He had to shake him several times before Sean even started to wake up, opened his eyes, and looked dully at Andrew.

"What's it?" he mumbled.

"Beasley's gone. Do you know where?"

Sean shook his head, closed his eyes, and started to go back to sleep.

"No, don't do that!" said Sara. "We've got to talk to you!"

Bending down, Andrew looked into Sean's eyes.

"He's not just sleepy," he said. "He's been drugged!"

"Drugged! But how? And by whom?"

"I don't know by whom, but this is how." He held up the bottle containing the sleeping draught that Dr. Reeves had left for Beasley and showed her that it was more than half empty. "It was probably put in his tea."

Sara picked up the teacup, smelled it, and nodded.

"I think it was. But who could have done it? Could it have been Beasley himself?"

The door opened, and Mrs. Wiggins bustled in carrying a tray.

"Good morning," she said cheerfully. "I wanted to see how you were, so I —" She looked at the empty bed and blinked. "Where's Mr. Beasley?"

"We don't know," said Sara. "We were worried about him, so we took turns sitting up with him. Sean had the last watch, and when we came in here a few minutes ago, he was asleep and Mr. Beasley was gone."

"He couldn't have left by himself!" said Mrs. Wiggins. "At least, he shouldn't have."

"No, he certainly shouldn't," said Andrew. "The whole thing's very strange because we think Sean's been drugged."

"Mr. O'Farrell?"

"Yes," said Sara. "With Mr. Beasley's sleeping medicine."

"But who could have given it to him?"

"We don't know," said Andrew. "But maybe Sean does. So do you want to give him Mr. Beasley's breakfast — particularly his tea — and see if that will help wake him up?"

"Yes, of course," said Mrs. Wiggins, setting down the tray. "What are you going to do?"

"We're going downstairs to see if we can find anything that will tell us how or why Beasley left."

They went downstairs and found both the front and

back doors still locked from the inside. The windows were all locked too, except the French doors that looked out on the garden.

"Matson always locks them when he locks up at night," said Sara.

"That means Beasley must have gone out that way," said Andrew.

"Which brings us back to the question we asked before, why?"

"Not just why, but how? He wasn't well enough to go off by himself at four in the morning."

"No."

"Of course," said Andrew slowly, "there's one thing we haven't discussed."

"What's that?"

"That note he got before when Dr. Reeves was here. The one Matson brought up."

Sara frowned, looking at him thoughtfully. "You think there may have been something in it that made him decide to leave?"

"Not only that, but whoever wrote it may have helped him."

"You're right."

They went out into the garden to see if there was anything there that could tell them a little more about what had happened, but there was nothing. When they got back upstairs, Sean was drinking the hot, strong tea that

Mrs. Wiggins had given him and seemed almost himself again.

"We did talk a little," he said in answer to their questions. "He woke up and said he was hot and asked me to open one of the windows," he nodded to it, "and to tie back the curtain."

"That's probably when he put the sleeping medicine in your tea," said Sara. "When you were busy with the window."

"He could have," said Sean. "But why did he do it?"

"That's what we've been asking ourselves," said Andrew. "That and where he is now. I think we should go look in his house and the shop, see if he's at either one. And if he's not . . . well, I've one other idea."

"All right," said Sean. "Get dressed and have your breakfasts, and I'll meet you downstairs."

"We'll be quick," said Sara. "And since we have a lot of ground to cover, do you think we could ask Fred to drive us, Mother?"

"Of course," said Mrs. Wiggins. "I'll see that he's ready."

Since there was nothing Fred liked better than to be involved in something that promised excitement, of course he was ready. They went first to Beasley's house, then to the shop. There was no sign of him at either place.

"Well, that's that," said Sean. "Now what?"

"What was your idea?" Sara asked Andrew.

"That we go to Scotland Yard and talk to Sergeant Tucker."

"That's what I hoped you'd say," said Sean. "I don't like going to the police and neither does old Beasley, but I think that under the circumstances it's certainly called for."

"It's about time you got around to deciding that," said Fred. "Get in, and I'll take you there."

He took them there by way of Kensington Road and Victoria Street, dropping them off at the Embankment entrance. They went through the gate and across the courtyard to the Yard's main entrance. The desk sergeant remembered Sara and Andrew, sent a note upstairs, and a few minutes later the three of them were knocking on the door of Wyatt's office. They were invited to come in, and Sergeant Tucker, sitting at his own small desk in a corner of the crowded room, looked up at them from the folder of notes he was reading.

"I knew that things were too quiet this morning," he said. "Nothing to do except nobble Jack the Ripper until his nibs gets here tomorrow. Then in you walk like the three weird sisters out of *Macbeth*. So tell me the worst. Is it the Crown Jewels that have been snatched from the Tower or the Elgin Marbles from the British Museum?"

"Neither," said Sara. "You're not even close."

"Then I'm puzzled. If it was just you and Andrew, nothing you could come here about would surprise me.

But when Mr. O'Farrell, an associate of that royal scamp, Beasley, comes here with you. . . . How is the old buzzard?"

"We don't know," said Andrew. "That's why we're here."

"Oh?" Tucker put down his folder and prepared to listen. "All right. Tell me."

They did — Sean telling the earlier parts of the story and Sara and Andrew the later ones. Tucker listened quietly, looking at each one in turn as he or she talked. He took no notes, but they all knew that he was not only listening but would remember everything that was said in all its details. He was silent for a moment when they had finished.

"It was just this morning that he left your place?" he said to Andrew. "A few hours ago?"

"That's right."

"How do you know he didn't go by himself — go because he wanted to go?"

"We think he probably did," said Andrew. "But why did he do it? Why did he go when he wasn't really well; and why didn't he say anything to us about it?"

"Why didn't he say anything to me at least?" said Sean. "Why did he knock me out with that sleeping draught of his?"

"What would you have said if he told you he was leaving?"

"I would have tried to talk him out of it. After all, he was still sick."

"Well, there you are. That's why he didn't say anything to you about it."

"But why did he want to leave?" asked Sara. "And where is he now?"

"Come on! You've been around the inspector and me enough to answer that. He left because he was worried, scared. And if he wanted you to know where he was going, he'd have told you."

"What do you think we should do about it?" asked Sean.

"Nothing."

"Nothing?"

"That's right. If I went to Missing Persons about it, they'd laugh at me. After all, he's only been gone for a few hours. And besides, it looks very much as if he's gone off on his own because he wanted to."

"You know very well that the whole thing's very rum," said Andrew.

"Yes, it is. There's a lot about it that I don't like. Your new stepfather gets back tomorrow. I don't know when he'll come in here, but whenever he does, I'll go over everything you've told me with him, and — Yes?" he said in response to a knock. "Come in."

A constable carrying a sheaf of papers came in, sketched an ironic salute to Tucker, handed him a note, and left.

"Good deal of slackness around here," muttered Tucker. "Some of these constables act as if this were a station house and not the Yard. The inspector's no spit and polisher, but just the same if he was here. . . ." He had been unfolding the note as he talked and now, glancing at it, "Thunderation!" he said. "Blast!" Putting down the note, he looked at his visitors. "The coves that were in Beasley's backyard were Indians?"

"Yes, they were," said Sara.

"All right. Then listen to me. This isn't jiggery-pokery. It's serious! And what I'm saying is not just friendly chit-chat. It's official! You keep away from anything that has anything to do with old Beasley! Is that clear?"

"What you're saying is clear," said Andrew. "But I'm afraid I don't know why you're saying it."

"The why is none of your business. You just do it! And if you've got any complaints, you can take them up with the inspector when he gets back. And now, clear out. I've got a lot to do."

"But, sergeant —" Sara began.

"Out!" he bellowed.

"Well, well," said Andrew when they were outside in the corridor. "I've never seen old Tucker like that."

"It was the note that did it," said Sara. "He was worried."

"I wonder what was in the note?" said Sean. "It must have had something to do with what we were talking about."

"There's no way we can find that out," said Andrew. "What was in the note, I mean. But . . . I didn't look at a paper this morning. Did either of you?" They shook their heads. "Let's get one."

They went down the stairs, across the courtyard, and out onto the Embankment. There was a newspaper seller on the corner of Bridge Street. Andrew bought an *Express*, and they stood there, near the Bridge Street bus stop, going through it. There was nothing that seemed at all relevant on the first two pages, and Andrew had skimmed page three and was about to turn to the next one when Sara said, "What about this?" and pointed to a small item on the bottom of the page. It was headed, *Murder in Westbourne Grove*.

They read it, standing huddled together. It concerned the body of a man that had been found in an alley off Chepstow Road. He had been strangled and robbed. At first glance there was nothing too unusual about it, but there were two things in the last sentence that Andrew found very interesting.

"This is the second murder of this sort that has taken place in the last few days," said the paper. "Does this signal the beginning of a new wave of garrotings, similar to the stranglings by the Indian Thugs, that took place here in London during the 1860's?"

"That could be it," said Andrew.

"Because it talks about Indian Thugs?" said Sean.

"Yes."

"But this last murder took place the day before yesterday. The note that Tucker got — the one that upset him so — must have been about something that happened since then."

"Suppose the note was about a *third* murder," said Sara, "one that the papers haven't written about yet. Wouldn't that get him upset?"

Sean whistled softly.

"Yes, it would," he said. "And it would get me pretty upset too. In fact, it has."

8

More Questions about Beasley

Dr. Reeves frowned.

"You've no idea of either why he left or where he is now?"

"No, none," said Andrew.

"It's very strange. And very disturbing. In a way, I blame myself for it."

"Why should you do that?" asked Sara.

"I said I would come back, and I didn't. I had an emergency at hospital that kept me until almost midnight, and I thought that was too late. But perhaps if I'd come back earlier. . . ."

"I don't think it would have made any difference," said Sean. "If he'd made up his mind to leave, he would have left whether you'd been to see him or not."

"And you're convinced that he did go of his own free will? That he wasn't coerced or abducted?"

"We haven't ruled it out," said Andrew. "But it seems more logical that he left on his own than that someone kidnapped him. There's that note he got during the afternoon, which may have told him something that alarmed him. And there's not much doubt that it was he who put that sleeping draught in Sean's tea."

"No, there isn't. You've no idea where he can be now?"

"No," said Sara. "We'll do some more looking for him this afternoon, but . . . Are you worried about him physically? I mean, is he in any danger because of whatever was wrong with him?"

"No. As I told you, I think he was given a drug. I'm still not sure what kind or how it was administered. But whatever, it gave him hallucinations, made him feel and act the way he did. And I assume that when he left here, he stopped taking the drug. But I still find the whole thing very upsetting. Inspector Wyatt is coming back tomorrow?" he said to Andrew.

"Yes. He and my mother get into Victoria Station a little before eleven in the morning."

"I assume you intend to tell him everything that has happened."

"We certainly do. I'm not sure we'll do it as soon as we meet him, but we'll try to do it sometime during the day."

"Very good. Tell him that I'm at his disposal, that I'll be glad to talk to him any time he'd like. And in the meantime, I'll continue with my own research, try to discover what kind of drug he was given and how."

Nodding to the two young people and Sean, Dr. Reeves left. He had arrived at the house just a few minutes after they returned from their visit to Sergeant Tucker at Scotland Yard and was as disturbed as they had been to discover that his patient was gone. And he was not the only one who was upset about it. The three had just gone into the parlor to discuss their next move when Matson knocked on the door and told them that Mr. Bannerji was there and would like to see them.

"Show him in," said Andrew, and a moment later Bannerji hurried in, looking even more agitated than Dr. Reeves.

"I met the good doctor as he was leaving," said Bannerji. "And when I asked him how our friend Beasley was, he told me he didn't know. That he was gone."

"It's true," said Andrew. "He has gone."

"Gone where? When did he go? And why?"

And so for the third time they went over the strange and puzzling events of the night and the morning — the events that led up to Beasley's disappearance.

Bannerji's first question was similar to the one that Dr. Reeves had asked.

"You've no idea where he's gone?"

"No, none."

"This is a bad — a very bad business. I am very afraid for him."

Andrew exchanged glances with Sara and Sean.

"Why afraid? Do you think he's in danger?"

"In very great danger."

"What kind of danger?"

"I would rather not say."

"We were just down to Scotland Yard," said Sara, "talking to a friend of ours who knows Beasley. He was upset, too, and we got the impression that he thought Beasley might be in danger from the garrotings that have been taking place here in London lately."

"That was very astute of your friend. Is he someone who works with Inspector Peter Wyatt?"

"Yes, he is," said Andrew. "How do you know of Inspector Wyatt?"

"In making inquiries into our friend Beasley's background, I discovered that he's an old friend of Inspector Wyatt. I also learned that you have some sort of connection with him, too."

"It's more than a connection," said Sara. "We've not only known him for some time, but just recently he married Andrew's mother."

"That was what I heard. They are away at the moment, are they not?"

"Yes," said Andrew. "But they'll be back tomorrow."

"Late tomorrow?"

"No, tomorrow morning, around eleven."

"Then may I ask a favor of you?" said Bannerji. "As

you can tell, I am very concerned about Mr. Beasley. Will you tell the inspector of that concern and also tell him that I have information that makes it imperative that I see him as soon as possible."

"We'll tell him," said Andrew. "How can he get in touch with you?"

"I am at present working with the East India Company," said Bannerji. "He can reach me there. But since the matter is so urgent, what I will do is stop by at Scotland Yard. If he can see me when I get there, splendid. If not, perhaps he will be good enough to tell me when he can see me."

"I'm sure he'll do that," said Sara. "We'll tell him he'll be hearing from you."

"You are very good," said Bannerji. "Good and brave and intelligent. With such friends, Beasley cannot possibly come to any harm."

And, bowing to them, he left.

"So he does know something," said Sean. "Why couldn't he tell us what it is?"

"Because he doesn't really know anything about us," said Sara. "If it is anything important, he'd want to tell it to someone official."

"I suppose that's true," said Sean. "Well, at least we know he's on the square. I mean, if he works for the East India Company and wants to see the inspector, he must be all right."

"He probably is," said Andrew. "Though I don't think we can take anything for granted. The question is, what do we do now?"

"It's almost lunchtime," said Sara. "Why don't we have lunch here and then make one more royal try to find Beasley?"

"I'm for the lunch part," said Sean. "I'm hungry. But where can we look that we haven't looked already?"

"I think we should try looking where we *have* looked before — at his house and at the shop. He may have gone to one or the other because he knows we've been there already and he won't expect us to come back."

"That's an idea," said Andrew. "All right. We'll give it a go."

And so after lunch — some cold gammon left from last night's supper — they sent word to Fred that if he felt up to it, they could use the carriage again. He came storming into the house to remind them that the madam — now Mrs. Wyatt — was coming home the next day and, after an absence of several weeks, had a right to expect her carriage to be looking like a royal coach. He had planned to put in the afternoon going over it, and here a pair of lolloping layabouts who could get around perfectly well on their own were expecting him to stop what he was doing, and so on. This was a scene that Sara and Andrew had often played before, and they knew their roles perfectly. So while Sean stared in surprise, the two young people apologized to Fred and told him that they'd take buses; and of course, when they left the house, the landau was waiting for them, looking if not royal, then at least ducal. And Fred's only question was where they wanted to go first.

They said Beasley's house, and he took them there. They went in, but there was no sign of Beasley. The people in the boarding house next door, however, appeared to have gotten over their fear and moved back in again.

They then asked Fred if he would take them to the shop, and he did. Sean unlocked the door, and they all went in. Again there was no sign of Beasley. Disappointed, they were just coming out when, with a creaking rumble, a dustman's cart drew up and, gray with ashes, Whispering Willie came around from the far side of it and up to them.

"Afternoon, Sean," he said in his hoarse, wheezing voice. "Afternoon, younkers. How goes?"

"Up and down like Tower Bridge," said Sean in the accepted response.

Willie nodded. "And what about old Beasley? He was sick last time I seen you. How is he?"

"We don't know. He's disappeared."

"What do you mean, disappeared?"

"I mean like took off, vanished, scarpered."

"Since when?"

"Last night or early this morning. We've been looking for him ever since."

"Why you doing that?" asked Willie, chuckling huskily. "The rozzers was probably after him, and he figured he'd better lie low for a bit."

"I know you mean that as a joke," Andrew said quietly. "But if the police are looking for him, it's not because of anything he's done but because they're worried about him, too."

"Well, spit in my eye and shut my box! You're not codding me, and he really is gone?"

"Yes."

"I'm sorry," he said quietly and sincerely.

"That's all right, Willie," said Sean. "I know it's hard to believe. It makes no more sense to us than it does to you. But, look, you get around. Will you keep your eyes open and let us know if you see anything that might be useful?"

"I'll do that all right. But look 'ee, I ain't known Beasley for long, but I do know 'ow many blue beans make five, and I can tell you this — don't you worry about the old chickaleary. He's going to be all right!"

And nodding with great conviction, he went up the street with his horse and cart, blowing an occasional plaintive blast on his small horn.

"You know," said Sara, "I think he meant that."

"Oh, he meant it all right," said Sean. "Old Beasley has a way of picking up with strange types, and Willie's one of the strangest. But there's no doubt that he likes Beasley."

"Has he been around here for long?" asked Andrew.

"Willie? No, only for about three or four weeks. He took over from a pair of really tired old culls. But, as you know, it doesn't take Beasley long to make a friend."

9

The Travelers Return

The Wyatts' train from Dover was due at Victoria Station at ten minutes of eleven. Andrew and Sara were there well before that and bought platform tickets so they could greet the returning travelers as soon as they arrived and not have to wait until they came through the barrier.

Andrew had been afraid that Sara might hesitate about coming with him, claiming that it was a family affair and she did not belong at that first meeting. But apparently Andrew and his mother had finally convinced her that she had every right to consider herself a member of the family. For, as Verna had pointed out, if Mrs. Wiggins had acted as foster-mother to Andrew when he first came to London and she, Verna, was away, then Verna should have the right to act in that same capacity toward Sara, now that Verna was back. As for Verna's relationship with Mrs. Wiggins, that was something else again, but equally strong. For it was based on mutual respect: Mrs. Wiggins' admiration for Verna as an actress and a person and Verna's appreciation of Mrs. Wiggins' warmth, loyalty, and qualities as a housekeeper.

The train came in on schedule and stopped with a clanking of couplings and much hissing of steam. Porters had been gathering for some time; since it was a boat train, it was one of the most important arrivals of the day. They moved along the platform looking for passengers who might require their services as the compartment doors began opening.

"There they are!" said Sara. "Peter, anyway."

Andrew had seen him, too, and together they hurried toward the first class compartment where Wyatt, casual but distinguished looking in a tweed coat and soft felt hat, was simultaneously signaling a porter and helping Verna down out of the compartment.

"Hello, Sara . . . Andrew," he said. But before they could return his greeting, Verna had thrown her arms around both young people and was kissing them in turn.

"Hello, Mother," said Andrew with sudden shyness.

"Hello yourself," said Verna, smiling at him. "I must say you look pretty well considering my absence."

"And you look just marvelous!" said Sara, looking first at her radiant face and then at the green velvet traveling outfit she was wearing with a matching bag and hat.

97

"You mean this?" said Verna, doing a sweeping and exaggerated turn as if she were modeling the suit. "Just a little something I picked up in Paris. After all, what else can one do in Paris?"

"Eat," said Wyatt. "Which we did also, to the point of satiation. And now, may I greet our welcoming committee also?" Bending down, he kissed Sara on both cheeks, then held out his hand to Andrew. "How are you?" he asked.

"Fine, sir."

"All goes well?"

"Why, yes, sir," said Andrew with just a suggestion of a pause between each of the words. Wyatt, skilled at noticing the faintest shades of expression, looked at him sharply.

"That's good," he said in a flat, neutral voice. "I take it that Fred's here."

"Outside," said Sara. "And waiting very impatiently, if I know him."

"Well, we can't have that," said Verna. "Are we ready?" she asked Wyatt, who glanced at the porter to make sure he had all their baggage on his barrow and nodded. "Forward, then."

Fred, standing in front of the gleaming landau, greeted the travelers with a grin and a flourish and began supervising the placing of the luggage.

"Do you mind if I don't come along with you, my

dear?" said Wyatt as he helped Verna into the carriage. "I'd like to stop off at the Yard for a few minutes."

"But you're not due back until tomorrow."

"I know. But I'd like to say hello to old Tucker, see if anything urgent's come up while we were away."

"All right. What about Andrew and Sara?"

"Why don't I take them with me? They'd probably like to say hello to Tucker, too. I'll give them lunch, and then we'll all come home together?"

Verna looked at him as keenly as he had looked at Andrew; then, apparently deciding that a policeman's wife does not ask any questions no matter what she suspects, she nodded.

"Very well. You realize, of course, that this is the first time we've been separated since we were married."

"I do. But it won't be for long."

He kissed her, closed the carriage door and, as it moved off, signaled to a waiting four-wheeler. He told the cabby to take them to the Yard, saw Sara and Andrew in and only then, when he had gotten in himself, did he say, "All right. What is it? What's wrong?"

"It's Beasley," said Andrew.

"What about him?"

"He's gone, disappeared."

"Tell me."

They did, telling him everything that had happened from the beginning. They finished just as the growler

99

drew up in front of the arched entrance to Scotland Yard. Wyatt had not said anything, asked a single question during their detailed account, and he did not say anything now. Getting out of the four-wheeler, he paid the cabby and led the way across the courtyard and into the large brick-and-stone building.

Wyatt nodded to the sergeant at the desk, who saluted and said, "I didn't think you'd be in today, sir. But someone else thought you might and said he'd wait for you." He nodded toward one of the benches off to the side where Sean sat.

"Hello, Sean," said Wyatt, going over to him. "How did you know I'd be coming here today?"

"I didn't. But I knew you were coming home, and I thought *if* by some chance you did come in, I'd like to see you, speak to you."

"All right. Andrew and Sara told me what's been happening, so I know why you're here. Let's go up to my office."

He led the way up the stairs, along a corridor, and opened the door of his office without knocking. Sergeant Tucker, at his desk with a pen in his hand, looked up without surprise.

"Well, well," he said. "The bridegroom has returned a day early. And," looking at Sean and the two young people, "unlike the rolling stone, he seems to have gathered a good deal of moss."

"There's at least one thing around here that hasn't changed," said Wyatt, "and that's the man who has a misquotation or a mixed metaphor for every occasion. How are you, sergeant?"

"Seeing as how what you said is undoubtedly uncomplimentary, I'd rather not answer that. I won't ask how you are because you look as blooming as a meadow in June, and I hope the new missus is the same?"

"She is, sergeant." Then, at a knock, "Yes? Come in." A constable opened the door and handed him a note. "Well," he said when he read it, "here's someone else who seemed to have a feeling that I might be coming in today."

"Is it Mr. Bannerji?" asked Andrew.

"Yes."

"He was very anxious to see you. He claims he has something important to tell you and said he'd stop by and, if you couldn't see him, perhaps you'd tell him when you would be able to."

"Well, if it's important, we should make it as soon as possible — like now. But not in this office. It's too crowded as it is. Is there any place else we can use, sergeant?" he asked Tucker.

"Superintendent Sawyer is away. I'm sure he wouldn't mind if you used his office."

"Fine. Would you bring Mr. Bannerji to the superintendent's office?" he said to the constable. "You'd better come, too," he said to Tucker. "And bring your notebook."

"Dizzifying this is," said Tucker, rising to his full and awe-inspiring height, "disturbing and discombobulating. Here I was expecting to have another day of rest before the hurricane struck, and instead — whisht! It's on us and we're off to the races without even having time to batten down the hatches."

"Was it you who wanted to know what a mixed metaphor was?" Wyatt asked Sara.

"No."

"Well, there, in any case, is a prime example of one. The hurricane is *not* upon us, sergeant. I am not yet back officially, but when someone says they have important information for us, I'd be derelict in my duty if I did not listen. Now let's go to Sawyer's office."

They followed him along the corridor, and he opened a door into a large corner office with two desks in it. Wyatt went around and stood behind the larger desk, Tucker took the smaller one, and Sara, Andrew, and Sean sat down in some straight chairs that were set against the wall. The door opened, and the constable ushered in Mr. Bannerji, who was dressed as neatly as he always was. In addition to his umbrella, he carried a bulging leather briefcase.

"Mr. Bannerji?" said Wyatt.

"Yes. You are Inspector Wyatt?"

"I am."

"I am more than pleased — I am honored to meet you," said Bannerji, bowing. "Am I correct in thinking you know who I am?"

"Yes. My young friends here," he nodded toward Andrew and Sara, "have told me about you."

"And that is all?" said Bannerji, somewhat distressed. "Have you not also had advices about me from India?"

"I believe our commissioner had a note from the district commissioner in Benares that mentioned you."

"Ah, good. He said he would write. In addition to all this, you can, if you wish, inquire at the East India Company about me. I am at present translating some of our sacred writing, the Vedas, for them."

"Why are you making such a point of your references?"

"Because what I want to talk to you about is of great importance and I wanted to make certain that there was no question about my background or bona fides."

"I see. And does what you wanted to talk to me about concern Mr. Beasley of Portobello Road?"

"It does." He glanced at Tucker, Sean, and the two young people. "I had, of course, expected to talk to you privately."

"Mr. O'Farrell, who works with Mr. Beasley, and my two young friends appear to have been involved with Mr. Beasley's illness and disappearance from the beginning. And Sergeant Tucker is a valued and trusted associate, who has worked with me for some time. So I cannot think of anything you can say to me that they should not hear."

"I must say I have been impressed by the intelligence and dedication of Mr. O'Farrell and your two young friends. And of course if that is the way you feel about it, then there is nothing more to be said. Shall I begin then?"

"Please do."

10

The Stranglers

"I think," said Bannerji, "that I had better begin with some background. Do you know who the dacoits are?"

"If they are, as I think, the same as the Thugs, I believe I do," said Wyatt. "But since it's probable that the others don't know, I suggest that you tell us whatever you think is necessary about them."

"Very well," said Bannerji. "I will start with the etymology of the word *thug*, which comes from the Sanskrit word *sthag*, which means 'to cover, conceal, deceive,' and go on with the story of the supposed origin of the Thugs."

"Supposed?"

"It is part of our Indian mythology, and whether it is true or not, it is firmly believed by many. It goes back to the days when Kali, the destroyer goddess and consort of Shiva, who was also known as Bhowani, was helping Shiva in his struggle against the demons who peopled the earth at that time. In a battle with one particular demon, Kali found that from every drop of his blood that was shed a new demon was born. In order to conquer, she created two disciples whom she instructed to kill her adversaries by strangling them so that no blood would be shed and no further demons arise. When the battle against the demons was finally won, in return for their help, she gave those disciples and their descendants the right to kill anyone they liked — as long as they did not spill any blood — and to keep the spoils they had gained from the murders."

"I see why you wanted to tell that story," said Wyatt. "You are giving us the religious basis for thuggee."

"Exactly. The worship of Kali or Bhowani was used by this particular sect as an excuse for murder for profit. That is one of the reasons the sect has been so immensely powerful, why it has existed for so long, and why it still exists today."

"You mean it still does exist today?" said Andrew.

"Yes, my young friend. It still does, even under the British rule. Or at least it did until just a short time ago. It went on for centuries under our own native rulers. And why not, when the profits from this religious killing were so enormous that protection could be bought from the highest authorities? It was not until Lord William Bentinck became governor general in the late 1820's that truly vigorous efforts were made to stamp it out. He thought it important enough to establish a Department of Dacoity and Thuggee as part of his government. And it was an agent of this department, Captain William — later Sir William — Sleeman who was able to end this criminal activity by penetrating the organization with several companions. Through their testimony and that of informers, more than three thousand Thugs were identified, brought to trial, and either imprisoned or hanged."

"Three thousand?" said Tucker.

"Yes, sergeant. That will give you some idea of the size of the organization. It's impossible to be certain how many victims this dreadful and murderous sect claimed, but Captain Sleeman estimated that for the previous three hundred years the Thugs killed about forty thousand men and women a year." He looked around at them. "You are shocked?"

"Shocked is not a strong enough word," said Wyatt. "Speechless would be more accurate. I knew something about the Thugs, but even I am astonished."

"But how did they do it?" asked Sara in an incredulous, horrified voice. "How *could* they do it, kill forty thousand people a year and not be caught?"

"First of all, they did not operate in the cities where there was a certain amount of law and police protection. They operated in the countryside, and their technique was simple. Individual members of a Thug gang would pose as guides, soldiers, priests — either Muslim or Hindu — anything that might be useful to a traveler. As I told you, the word *thug* means deceiver. The leader of the gang — in whatever role he had chosen — would offer his services to a merchant or rich traveler, involve other members of his group as porters, mule or camel drivers, cooks, or servants. Then, when they were in an isolated spot, they would kill their victims, bury them, and divide their money and goods."

"This killing," said Tucker, "it was done by strangling?"

"The police officer's interest in method, the *modus operandi*," said Bannerji with a slight smile. "No, sergeant. Though they were called the Stranglers, they did not always kill by strangulation. The ritual *rumal*, or noose, was actually a silk scarf. Silver coins were knotted into one corner of it to give it weight. When a skilled *bhottote*, or strangler, used it, he would whip it out of his belt with one fluid motion. The weight of the silver coins would carry it around his victim's neck and, with a practiced twist, the Thug would break his victim's neck, killing him instantly." Then, as Tucker looked significantly at Inspector Wyatt, "Did you have a special reason for asking that question?"

"Yes," said Tucker. "I'll tell you why in a little while."

"You began by saying that you wanted to talk to us about our friend, Beasley," said Andrew.

"I did. And I will now get to him," said Bannerji. "By the late 1830's the Thugs had virtually been wiped out. But their roots went so deep that it was difficult to destroy them completely. About ten years ago there was a revival of their activities. Their operations were not nearly as extensive as they had been before, but enough murders were being committed to alert the authorities. They did what they had done so successfully before — found someone who could penetrate the Thug organization as Captain Sleeman had and bring its leaders to justice. Again the tactic was successful, and a little over a year ago several hundred important Thugs were brought to trial and either executed or imprisoned."

"And who was the man who penetrated the organization this time?" asked Wyatt.

"We do not know," said Bannerji. "At least, I don't. It is generally believed that he was an Anglo-Indian, an Englishman who was brought up in India and could pass as either a Hindu or a Muslim. But aware of the danger he was in — for any remaining Thugs would have sworn an oath to kill him — the authorities kept his identity a secret. He testified wearing a mask and under an assumed name. Not only that, but when the trial was over, he and a man who worked closely with him — a Muslim named Amir Ali — were at once sent out of the country."

"Where are they now?" asked Sean.

"I can tell you where Amir Ali is," said Bannerji. "As I'm sure Inspector Wyatt can, too. He's in the British cemetery in Alexandria."

"You mean he's dead?" said Sara.

"Yes. Somehow the remaining Thugs discovered his true identity and the one under which he was traveling. They caught up with him when his ship stopped in Alexandria, killed him there."

"And the Englishman?" asked Andrew.

"Disappeared. Until that time he had been relying on the authorities to keep his identity hidden and protect him. When his friend and associate, Amir Ali, was killed, he must have thought that he could no longer count on the authorities. That he would be better off on his own. So he dropped out of sight, disappeared without a trace."

"I still don't see what this has to do with Mr. Beasley," said Sean.

"Don't you?" said Bannerji. "I venture to suggest that Inspector Wyatt does."

"I think I know what you have in mind," said Wyatt. "You think that this mysterious Anglo-Indian agent came here to England, got in touch with Beasley, and Beasley helped him hide, disappear. You think further that all these strange things have been happening to Beasley because members of the Thug gang, who are now here in England, believe this too and have been trying to find out from him who this Mr. X is and where they can find him."

"Exactly. You have hit the nail squarely on the head, as I thought you would."

"The reason I asked before just how these Thugs

killed," Tucker said to Wyatt, "is because during the past week we've had three murders in which the victims were robbed. In each case, though we called them garrotings or stranglings, the victim's necks were broken."

"I suspected that," said Bannerji. "If there were Thugs here in London and they needed money, they would obtain it exactly as they would have in India."

"Yes," said Wyatt. "May I ask what your relationship with Beasley was — when and how you met him?"

"Of course," said Bannerji. "And in this Mr. O'Farrell will bear me out. I happened to walk past his shop about three weeks ago, saw a statue of Kali in the window, and immediately went in to talk to him. I asked him if he knew what it was. He did and he also knew that it was old and authentic, but he refused to tell me where he had gotten it. Is this true, Mr. O'Farrell?"

"As far as I know, it is," said Sean.

"I then told him a little about Kali's — or Bhowani's — connection with the Thugs and warned him that it might be dangerous to show it openly as he had been doing. He shrugged, clearly skeptical of what I had said, and I left. When I stopped by again about ten days ago, however, the statue was gone. He would not tell me what had happened to it, and he was clearly a very frightened man."

"What do you think happened in the meantime?" asked Wyatt.

"I think that during that time the unknown Anglo-

Indian you called Mr. X arrived in London and, for some reason, got in touch with him. I think that Beasley helped him in some way and, if nothing else, knows who he is. The Thugs who are here in London trying to find Mr. X must have suspected this, too, and have been trying to find out exactly what Beasley knows. When Beasley finally realized the danger he was in, he decided to disappear in order to protect himself."

"I don't know all the details of his disappearance yet," said Wyatt, "but how do you know he went off on his own? How do you know that the Thugs have not captured him?"

"That is a possibility. I did not mention it because I do not like to think the worst in any situation. And this would be the worst. For if the Thugs have indeed captured him, after they have learned what they want to know from him, they will kill him."

"Then we'd better hope that your first thought was the correct one," said Wyatt. "Thank you very much for coming here, Mr. Bannerji, for your interest in this matter, and for the information you have given us. I can reach you at the East India Company on Leadenhall Street?"

"You can, sir," said Bannerji, rising. "I am on my way there now."

"I am not yet back officially," said Wyatt. "But I will be tomorrow, and I will then go into the whole matter very thoroughly. If I turn up anything that I think will interest you or I need your help again, I will get in touch with you."

"Thank you, sir. It was a pleasure — and an honor — to meet you." And bowing politely to all of them, Bannerji left.

"All right," said Wyatt. "Our young irregulars here, Sara and Andrew, gave me the short version of everything that's been happening. I'd like them to go over it again in more detail, and I'd like you to add anything you think necessary, Sean."

They did as he asked, and occasionally, as Wyatt had requested, Sean interrupted or added something. Again Wyatt listened quietly, asking only a few questions. One of them concerned Dr. Reeves. He wanted to know if he had come up with a firm diagnosis of Beasley's condition. When he heard that, as far as Sara, Andrew, and Sean knew, he hadn't, he told Tucker to make a note that he wanted to talk to Reeves. The other question concerned the room in the St. John's Wood house in which Beasley had been staying before he disappeared. Was there anything strange or different about it, he wanted to know.

Andrew, Sara, and Sean looked at one another, thinking about it.

"The one thing that seemed a little odd to me," said Andrew finally, "is that when he asked Sean to open a window, he only wanted him to open one window and tie back one curtain."

"That's true," said Sean. "When I wanted to open a second window and tie back that curtain, he told me not to."

Wyatt nodded, swinging his chair around and looking out the window at the Thames where a tug was pulling a string of lighters upstream. Sara studied him, frowning.

"There's something rum about this," she said. "Beasley was your friend long before he was ours. You introduced us to him and we know you like him, but somehow you don't seem terribly upset at what's happened to him. Is it because you know something that we don't?"

"What can I know when I just got back to London?"

"I don't know," said Andrew, "but Sara's right. You either know something or you've guessed something. I'll bet you know what's happened to him, maybe even where he is."

"That's very flattering. Do you think I'm a magician, a psychic, or the Sleuth of all Sleuths?"

"If you mean by that, the best detective in England, the answer is, yes. Sometimes."

"I repeat, that's very flattering, and it's nice to be appreciated by two such illustrious colleagues, but —" He broke off at a knock. Tucker went to the door and came back with a telegram, which he gave to Wyatt. Wyatt read it and put it in his pocket without commenting on its contents.

"I believe I promised you lunch, didn't I?"

"Yes, you did," said Sara.

"Well, it's getting late. Why don't the two of you go ahead to The White Stag and get a table for us — the one in the bay window if possible. I want to talk to Sean and Sergeant Tucker; Sean and I will be along soon."

Sara and Andrew looked at him, then at Tucker and Sean. They did not look at one another, but each knew what the other was thinking. Then they got up and left.

II

The White Stag

The White Stag was one of Wyatt's favorite restaurants. Sara and Andrew had been to it several times with him. They left the Yard by the rear entrance, the one notables or officials who don't want to be seen and recognized used, and walked up Cannon Street toward Bridge Street. Frank, one of the waiters who knew them, saw them come in.

"Is the inspector back?" he asked.

"Just got back. He'll be along soon," said Andrew.

"Ah. He'll be wanting his old table then."

Moving quickly, he cut off four Foreign Office types who were on their way to the table in the bay window, explained that it was reserved and, after turning them over to another waiter, settled Sara and Andrew there.

"How many of you will there be?" he asked.

"Four, I think," said Sara.

"And you'll want to wait till the others get here before you order."

"If you don't mind."

"Don't mind at all. Tell the inspector we've got steak-and-kidney pie today. If he's just back from foreign parts like I think he is, that's what he'll want after all that fancy, saucy, garlicky food."

"Probably. It's what I want anyway," said Andrew.

"And I do, too," said Sara. "All right," she continued as Frank went off. "Go ahead."

"With what?"

"What you were saying. I agree with what you said so far. I don't think your honorable stepfather is as worried about old Beasley as we've been, and I think the reason he's not is because he's got a pretty good idea of what happened to him."

"I know I said that, and I think it's true; but I'll be dashed if I know *how* he knows."

"Well, he can only know it from what we told him, so let's go over it. What were the things he seemed most interested in and asked questions about?"

"The first one was about the note Beasley got the afternoon before he disappeared. He wanted to know if we'd seen it, knew who it was from, or what was in it."

"And of course we didn't see it," said Sara.

"Right. The other thing he was interested in was Beasley having Sean tie back just one curtain, but —" He broke off. "That's it."

"When you put the two things together like that, yes. I think it is. The note must have been from someone who said, if you want to get away and need help, signal me by tying back one curtain in your room. He *did* signal him, and whoever sent him the note *did* help him get away, so the chances are he's safe somewhere."

"Chances are. But we can't be sure of it. The next question is why he sent us here and kept Sean there."

"Because he wanted to talk to him and didn't want us around when he did."

"That's obvious. But why? Sean doesn't know anything that we don't know. At least, I don't think he does."

"I don't think he does either. That means Peter must have wanted to tell him something. Was it something he wanted him to do?"

"Probably. The question is, what was it? And who helped Beasley?" They stared at one another. "Come on, Sara, think! If Peter was able to figure it out, we should be able to."

"That's not true. He *is* a little older and more experienced than we are and, since he's at the Yard, he may have information that we don't have."

"That's so. And I suppose we ought to allow for the possibility that he may be just a little smarter than we are."

"What are you saying?" said Sara with pretended incredulity.

"I know," said Andrew, smiling. "I don't really think that's possible either, but ... you know what? Tomorrow, just for fun, I'd like to see if we can't do a little more about this — either find Beasley or figure out what it is Peter wants Sean to do."

"Peter won't like it. That's probably why he didn't want us around when he talked to Sean."

"He didn't tell us to stay out of it, did he?"

"He probably thought we'd have sense enough to know that without his saying anything about it. Those Thugs sound like an awfully scary crew. Still, I suppose if we're careful. . . ."

At this point Wyatt and Sean came in, and they talked no more about it. They all had steak-and-kidney pie as Frank had thought they would, and then Sean left to go back to the shop.

Wyatt and the two young people took a four-wheeler home where, under Verna's supervision, their bags were being unpacked so that she and Wyatt could begin distributing the presents that they had brought home — not just for Andrew, Sara, and Mrs. Wiggins — but apparently for almost everyone they knew.

That evening Lawrence Harrison, the manager who had produced all the plays in which Verna had appeared, came for dinner with his wife and was regaled with tales about the trip, which seemed to have been everything that everyone had expected it to be.

When Sara and Andrew went up to bed, the travelers had only reached Venice in their account — with their stays in Florence and Rome still to come.

12

The Dust Yard

The next morning Andrew dressed carefully: carefully in the sense of thoughtfully, rather than in the sense in which the phrase is usually used. For he put on his oldest clothes — a pair of patched trousers and a jacket he had outgrown more than a year before. And instead of his school cap, he put in his pocket a deplorable tweed hat that he sometimes wore in the rain.

Verna would have had something to say about the way he was dressed if she had seen him, but she never came down for breakfast, and Wyatt was too busy reading the morning *Times* and getting ready for his first official day at the Yard to notice. Sara, on the other hand, looked as neat as she always did. But after Wyatt left — and after she had told her mother that she and Andrew were going out and would not be home for lunch — she told Andrew to go ahead and slipped upstairs. When she joined him walking toward Wellington Road, she was wearing a dress that was a little too small for her and very faded from many washings.

"I remember that dress," said Andrew. "It's the one you wore when we went boating in Regent's Park and you fell overboard."

"I never fell overboard," she said indignantly. "I got wet from the way you were rowing. And when we got home, Mum told me it was time I got rid of it and to put it in with the things she was sending to the Salvation Army."

"But you didn't."

"No. I thought it might come in useful some day, just like the things you're wearing. And, as you see, it has."

"Yes. We're not exactly disguised, but at least we won't be as noticeable as we usually are if we're going where I think we are."

"Which is where?"

"Well, I thought we might begin by going to Portobello Road and talking to Sean. If he knows anything, and I think he does, he might just tell us about it."

"I doubt it. We agreed that Peter sent us ahead to the restaurant because he didn't want us to hear what he was going to say to Sean, and he would have told Sean that. But I suppose it's worth a try."

They took a bus to Baker Street, changed for one that took them west past the trees, grass, and fountains of Hyde Park and got to Portobello Road at about the time the shops were opening up. Not Beasley's shop, however.

There was no sign of Sean, and as they tried to decide whether to wait or go looking for him, there was a low, hoarse hoot, and Whispering Willie appeared further down the street. He came toward them, leading his sway-backed horse and blowing an occasional blast on his small horn. It was clearly just as effective as the traditional cry of "Dust ho!" or "Dust oy-eh!" for shopkeepers whose dustbins were not already out, brought them out now. Sara and Andrew watched as he came up the street toward them, dumping the dustbins into his basket, carrying the basket to the cart, climbing the ladder he had rested against the side of the cart, and emptying the basket.

He raised a hand in salutation when he reached them, said "Wotcher, younkers," in his hoarse, wheezing voice and plodded on up the street.

"He's working alone," said Andrew, watching him. "Don't dustmen usually work in pairs?"

"Usually," said Sara. "But it means more money for him if he works alone. Then he doesn't have to divide what he gets with anyone else."

"But he has to work a lot harder if he does everything himself. If he took it a little easier, maybe he'd get rid of that sore throat of his." He was silent for a minute, looking after Willie. "I've been thinking," he said slowly. "Do you remember what he said the last time we saw him, when we told him Beasley had disappeared?"

"He said . . . didn't he say, don't worry about the old

something or other — that he was going to be all right?"

"That's right. And you said you had a feeling he meant it."

"Well, I did. I think he likes Beasley."

"I'm sure he does. The thing is, did he say Beasley was going to be all right because he *hoped* he would be, or did he *know* he was going to be because he knew where he was?"

Sara whistled softly, thoughtfully.

"Every once in a while you do get an interesting idea," she said.

"Thanks. Do you know anything about dustmen — where they go with their loads, what they do with them, where they live?"

"I think they take what they collect to a place called a dust yard. But I don't know what that means."

"Are you interested in finding out?"

"You've made me interested."

"Let's go then."

They had never actually shadowed anyone before, but they had heard enough talk about it from Peter Wyatt and Sergeant Tucker so that they understood the general theory, which was: be inconspicuous, but not conspicuously inconspicuous. In other words, don't try so hard not to be noticed that everyone notices you.

The first thing they did was separate, one walking on one side of the street, the other on the other side. And they took turns watching their quarry. Andrew would hang back, looking into a shop window, actually going into a shop or sitting down on a step to adjust the laces on his boot while Sara drifted along, keeping her eye on Willie. Then, when she had gone several blocks, Andrew would amble past her and take the lead in watching while she hung back. Of course, since Willie knew them, none of this would have done much good if he had been suspicious and looked around to see if he were being followed. But apparently he wasn't the least bit suspicious and just kept on with his hard, dusty work.

Willie continued with his collecting, going north and slightly west for well over an hour. Then, when his cart was full, he took his shaggy, shambling horse by the reins and led him a little faster in that same direction. Finally he came to some open, scrubby land and headed for a fenced-in area that was on the edge of the Grand Union Canal.

Sara and Andrew hung back until he had disappeared into the fenced-in area, then followed again, slowly and cautiously. When they reached the open gate through which Willie had gone, they peered in and realized that this must be a dust yard. In the center of the large, open area was a pile of ashes, cinders, and other things, onto which Willie was emptying the contents of his cart. Around this pile were eight or more men, women, and children — all as dirty as Willie — who took material from this center pile, sifted it through sieves and screens, and separated it into different piles. One of these contained broken bricks, cinders, and clinkers. Rags were placed on another pile; and bones, metals, bottles, old boots and shoes each had a separate pile. And finally, of course, there was one pile for the wet garbage. Evidently each of these categories of waste had its own use and could be sold.

They watched as Willie finished emptying his cart onto the large central pile, then led his horse over to a group of sagging, dilapidated wooden buildings that stood on the far side of the dust yard near the edge of the canal. He filled a bucket of water from a hand pump, gave it to his horse, and went into one of the buildings.

"Do you think that's where he lives?" asked Sara.

"Probably," said Andrew.

There was no doubt that people did live in the run-down houses, probably the people who worked in the dust yard. While Willie was emptying his cart, a woman carrying a baby had come out of one of the houses, called to the heavy, bearded man who seemed to be in charge, and he had nodded and waved to her.

"If he does live there, he may not come out again," said Sara.

"I think he will. It's still early. He could probably collect another load before lunchtime. Let's wait awhile and see."

Sara nodded, and Andrew proved to be right for, about ten minutes later, Willie came out again, untied his horse and, saying something to the bearded man, came toward them. Sara and Andrew stepped behind some empty barrels and boxes piled up beside the dust-yard gate and watched as Willie left, leading his patient horse across the scrubby ground and back toward the paved streets.

"It would be interesting to know what goes on in those buildings," said Andrew thoughtfully. "He didn't stay in there long enough to cook anything and eat or even to rest properly. But he was there long enough to talk to someone."

Sara looked at him sharply. "That's not as dim as some of your ideas," she said. "All right. You stay here. I'll go look."

"Why you? It might be dangerous."

"How can it be in daylight with people around? And it's got to be me because I can make myself look right and talk right and you couldn't, not in a million years. Watch!"

She kicked off her shoes — old by her standards, but still too good for what she had in mind — and scuffled her bare feet in the dirt so that they looked as if they hadn't been washed in weeks. She moistened a finger, rubbed it in the dirt, and dabbed and streaked it judiciously on her face. Unbraiding her hair, she tangled and snarled it. Then, slumping a little so that her dress hung even more awkwardly, she thrust out her jaw aggressively and said in nasal, rasping Cockney, "Got your eye full, Nosey?"

Those were the first words she had said to him when they had met some years before; she had been a street urchin then, living in Dingell's Court on the fringe of the slums near Edgeware Road. Andrew shook his head in wonderment at the way she had changed herself back into that girl with no makeup or costume, but only with her natural dramatic talent and the skills she had learned in her brief experience on the stage.

"All right," he said. "Go ahead. But if you're not back in a reasonable time, I'm coming after you."

"Righty-ho, chum," she said. "Ta-ta!"

And she went in through the gate and started across the dust yard in a shambling walk, pausing occasionally to kick something out of her way or wipe her nose on her bare arm. The bearded man and the sievers and sifters working around the central dust pile barely glanced at her as she went around them and toward the houses near the canal. The blowsy woman who had come out carrying the baby, came out again carrying a bucket of soapy water that she emptied, then stood there as Sara went up to her and began asking something. Andrew didn't know what she was saying but, whatever it was, the woman listened patiently but finally shook her head. Sara's shoulders slumped. Even at a distance Andrew could sense her disappointment. Then she thanked the woman and moved off. She didn't leave the yard, however. Instead, in typical childlike fashion, she drifted over to the bank of the canal, picked up a clinker and threw it into the muddy brown water, then went on along the canal bank until she disappeared behind the cluster of houses.

Andrew waited, and as time went by, the waiting became more and more difficult. He had not minded when he could watch Sara and see that she was safe. But he did not like it at all when she was out of sight. He had about made up his mind that he would go in and look for her when she reappeared on the other side of the clump of houses. Waving to the woman, who must have been looking out of one of the windows, she started across the dust yard toward the gate. Her progress seemed as casual and aimless as ever but, knowing her, Andrew sensed her hidden excitement. Just before she reached the open gate, he stepped out from behind the boxes where he'd been waiting and, eyes bright with excitement, she jerked her chin at him, indicating that he should start back toward town. He did, walking slowly across the open, scrubby wasteland while she pulled on her shoes and came hurrying after him.

"We were right," she said under her breath when she caught up with him. "He's there!"

"Beasley?"

"Yes. I talked to that woman who came out, said I was looking for work for me mum. That she'd do anything, washing if that was needed, or what about helping out in the dust yard? But the woman said there was nothing. So I thanked her and went off to the edge of the canal and worked my way behind the houses."

"I saw you."

"The woman lived in the first house. The second was the one Whispering Willie went into. Pieces of canvas hung over the back windows, but I was able to peek through a hole in one of them and there, in a little room, was Beasley!"

"What was he doing?"

"He was stretched out on a bed, smoking one of those terrible cigars of his and reading a book."

"Did he look all right?"

"He looked fine, better than any of the times we saw him since you came down from school."

Andrew whistled thoughtfully through his teeth.

"What do you think we should do?" Sara asked.

"Well, we should certainly tell Peter, though, as we agreed yesterday, he may very well know. But while we're on our way, I think we should stop off at the shop and talk to Sean, see if we can find out if *he* knows. And, if he doesn't, tell him we know Beasley's all right without necessarily telling him how we know and where he is."

"That makes sense," said Sara.

As she walked, she combed her hair with her fingers and braided it again, then when they passed a horse trough, wet her handkerchief and cleaned her face. By the time they reached Beasley's shop, she looked almost as clean as she had when she had first left the house.

The shop seemed closed and, when they tried the door, they found it locked. As they stood there uncertainly, the wispy, gray-haired man from the shop next door stuck his head out and said, "Want Sean?"

"Yes," said Sara.

"I'm pretty sure I saw him go in a while ago," he said. "Who don't you try knocking?"

"Thanks," said Andrew.

He knocked, and the curtain in back of the shop window moved slightly as if someone were looking out at them; then the lock turned, and the door opened. Sara went in, and Andrew followed.

As soon as he was inside, he knew something was wrong. The door slammed shut and was locked again. Strong hands seized him but before he could see whose they were, a cloth was wrapped around his face as a blindfold, then pushed into his mouth, gagging him. He was pushed to the floor, and his hands and feet were tied. From the scuffling sounds he heard, he knew that Sara was being treated the same way. Before he was really aware of what was happening to him — and of course before he had a chance to struggle — he was bound and helpless.

13

Captured

Clearly they had walked into a trap. There was no point in trying to decide who their captors were or whether they should have expected capture and could have avoided it. The one thing Andrew felt he could do was keep his wits about him and try to determine where they were being taken so that, if they had a chance, they could escape.

He was picked up by two people — one at his head and the other at his feet — and carried out the back way into the alley behind the shop. How did he know it was the back way and not the front? Because he felt the curtain that separated the back of the shop from the front brush against him as he was carried past it. Besides, no one would dare carry him bound and gagged into Portobello Road in broad daylight. The alley was different. It ran behind the shop and could not be seen from the street.

A horse stamped and snorted. A carriage door was

opened, he was lifted and set down on a seat. Someone was already sitting there, to his left. Was it Sara? At that moment, someone else was lifted into the carriage and set down on his right. This seemed like someone small and was probably Sara. But, if that were so, who was the third person to his left? Sean? That was possible. He'd have to wait and see not only who their captors were, but who their fellow captive was. Someone got into the carriage with them, sitting on the seat opposite. Someone outside said something in a language that was not English; the carriage door closed, and the carriage moved off.

Andrew tried to determine their route, but it wasn't easy. The alley ran north and south, but he wasn't sure which way they were headed, and therefore which way they were traveling. They had left the alley and were out in the street now — he could tell that from the sound of the wheels on the cobbles — but again he couldn't tell which way they were going.

Sara, sitting next to him, was wiggling a little. If he knew her, she was trying to free her hands. And, given a little time, he was sure she could. But the man sitting opposite them must have noticed what she was doing, too.

"No," he said, shaking her. "Must not do."

He had a deep voice and spoke with a slight accent. Whoever he was, he was not English. By now Andrew had lost all track of where they might be. He would have to try to determine that from what he could see whenever they got to where they were going. They traveled for about another ten minutes, rumbled over a bridge, made a sharp left turn and, after another five minutes or so, stopped.

The carriage door opened. First Sara and then he was lifted out. A knife sawed at the rope that tied his ankles.

"Feet now free," said the voice that had spoken before as the rope fell away. "Walk."

Someone held his elbow, guiding him, and he walked through a small garden — he heard leaves rustling and felt them brush against him — into a house, up a stair, and into a room that he felt was rather large. The knife now cut the rope that tied his hands behind him. The cloth that covered his eyes was removed and so was his gag. He blinked and looked around. He was in, as he had thought, a large room that was quite bare. Sara was with him. The third captive, rubbing his wrists and scowling angrily, was not Sean but Mr. Bannerji.

His eyes widened when he saw them.

"My dear young friends!" he said. "I hope you don't mind if I call you that. Are you all right?"

"Yes," said Sara. "Who are these people?"

Andrew turned and looked at them, too. There were five men in the room, all Indians. Three of them seemed to be seamen. Their tightly twisted turbans were somewhat soiled. They wore dark jerseys and patched canvas trousers. One of the others, shorter and slighter than Bannerji, was dressed in European clothes, but clothes of a distinctly foreign cut. The last man, older, taller, and more imposing than the others, wore a white turban and a long, white robe.

"I don't know who they are," said Bannerji, "but I think I can guess."

"I am sure you can," said the man in the European clothes. "I am Chunder Das and this is Ananda Lal."

He did not bother to introduce the three seamen — clearly they were of no importance — but Ananda Lal, the tall man in the white robe, bowed gravely to them.

"Why have they brought us here?" asked Andrew.

"That is the next thing we must find out," said Bannerji. And speaking in a firm, clear voice, he asked a question in what was probably Hindustani. Chunder Das answered him in the same tongue.

"They say they are sorry and *not* sorry that they kidnapped you," said Bannerji. "They were waiting in the shop because they wanted Mr. Beasley's assistant, Sean. Which of course is why I went there, and I imagine why you went there, too."

"Why did you want Sean?" asked Andrew.

"I suspect for the same reason you did. To find out if he had any word from our friend, Mr. Beasley. When I knocked on the door, they opened it, gagged me, and tied me up. A few minutes later, you knocked, and they served you the same way."

"Are they Thugs?" asked Sara. "Members of the gang you told us about at Scotland Yard?"

"You have been to Scotland Yard?" said Chunder Das.

"Yes, I have," said Bannerji defiantly.

Chunder Das said something in Hindustani to his white-robed companion, then turned his attention to Bannerji again, speaking to him with angry passion. Bannerji answered him, and Chunder Das said, "That is no concern of yours! Speak to them and tell them what they must do. And remember that I speak English, too. Not as well as you, but well enough to know if you are saying what we have told you to say."

"Very well," said Bannerji. Then, turning to Sara and Andrew, "As you probably gathered, we have been having an argument. I have been telling them that they are not in some remote part of India where the law does not reach. They are in England, the home of Anglo-Saxon law and the country with the best police force in the world, and they cannot do what they have been doing. They say that they are doing what they must do and insist that I tell you what they want. And that is for you to help them find our friend Beasley."

Sara and Andrew looked at one another.

"How can we help them?" asked Andrew. "As you know, we've been looking for him ourselves."

"They know that," said Bannerji. "And they do not think you know where he is. But they think that your friend Inspector Wyatt may know."

"If he does — and I don't know why they think he does — why should he tell them?"

"Because you will ask him to. They want you to write

a note to him saying that you and your friend, Miss Sara here, are prisoners and the price of your release is the information they want."

"And if we refuse?"

"You will not refuse," said Chunder Das who had been following the exchange carefully. "You will not refuse because you will be very sorry if you do, and it will do you no good. Because if you do not write the note, we will write it ourselves, saying we are holding you and what we want."

"You really think you can get away with that?" said Sara. "That you can make Inspector Wyatt do what you want?"

"Yes, my dear child, I think we can," said Chunder Das. "Because we have reason to believe that you and your young friend here are very important to him."

"Well, it will be interesting to see what comes of it," said Sara. "But, in the meantime, you're not planning to starve us, are you?"

"Starve?"

"Yes. It's lunchtime, and I'm very hungry. Aren't you?" she asked Andrew.

"Yes, I am."

"Oh, yes," said Chunder Das. He spoke rapidly to the man called Ananda Lal, who nodded. "We will feed you," he said to Sara. "Do you eat curry?"

"Yes, of course."

"Good." He spoke curtly to the three seamen, who

salaamed and left. "You will stay here," he said to Bannerji. Then he and Ananda Lal left also.

"That was well done," said Bannerji. "I assume you said what you did to give us time to talk and think."

"Partly," said Sara. "And partly because I *am* hungry."

"In the meantime," said Andrew, "let's see if we can figure out where we are and if there's anything we can do to escape."

He had been looking around the room ever since his blindfold had been taken off. It was a large room that had probably once been a back parlor. It was empty now except for some mats and cushions in one corner. He walked over to the windows and looked out. There was a narrow garden in back of the house and beyond that were the brown and muddy waters of a canal.

"Do you know where we are?" asked Bannerji.

"Yes," said Andrew. "That's the Grand Union Canal, which runs into the Regent's Canal. We're somewhere between Wormwood Scrubs and the branch of the canal that runs south to the Paddington Basin."

"What's that?" asked Sara, pointing.

Just to the right of the house was a dock and several sheds set close to the edge of the canal. A large steam launch was tied up to the dock, apparently with steam up, for faint puffs of smoke were rising from its tall stack.

"Looks like a boatyard," said Andrew. "There are quite a few along the canal. They rent out boats as well build and repair them."

"Well, whatever it is, it seems to have some connection with the people here."

Looking out, Andrew saw what she meant. A weather-beaten, gray-bearded seaman wearing boots, a short dark jacket, and a peaked cap was walking up the path from the boatyard to the garden in back of the house.

"Ahoy!" he called as he reached the garden. "Anyone about?"

A door immediately under the window from which they were watching opened, and Chunder Das stepped out.

"Good morning, Captain Clemson," he said. "Or should I say good afternoon?"

"Well, it's well after eight bells, but you can call it what you like. What I came up for was to see if you've got any word for me."

"No, captain. Not yet."

"Oh? My boy said you'd had visitors, and I thought maybe that was what you were waiting for."

"No, captain. However, it shouldn't be long now, so just keep the steam up in your launch and be patient."

"Long as I'm being paid for it, I don't mind. I'll stand by." And saluting Chunder Das, he turned and went back down the path to the boatyard.

"What was all that?" asked Sara.

"I do not know," said Bannerji, "except that this British captain seems in some way to be in league with my compatriots. But what is much more important is what you intend to do."

"About what?" asked Andrew.

"The demand of Chunder Das that you write a note to Inspector Wyatt, telling him that we are prisoners and he must give Chunder Das and the others whatever information he has about our friend Beasley."

"I don't think we should do it," said Andrew. "Do you, Sara?"

"I've been thinking about it, and I'm not sure. The only reason for doing it would be if we could put something in the note that would help him find us."

"Do you think you could?" asked Bannerji.

"We might be able to. On the other hand, once he realizes what's happened to us — which will be as soon as he gets a note from them or from us — he'll start looking for us anyway, so it doesn't really matter."

"But it does matter," said Bannerji gravely. "I am afraid you are not taking this seriously enough. These people are bad — very bad. If they are, as I think they are, Thugs, then they have killed many times in India and probably here, too. As long as you are in their power, you are in danger, and I would advise you to do anything they ask you to do in order to get away from them."

"If we are in danger," said Andrew, "and I suppose we are, then Beasley and Mr. X, the British agent you think he's trying to protect, would be in even more danger if these people found them. Well, I'm not going to save my skin by destroying someone else."

"But it's not just your own skin that you should be

thinking about," said Bannerji. "What about Miss Sara here?"

"I wouldn't let him do anything to save me that would put old Beasley or Mr. X in danger," said Sara.

"You are making a mistake," said Bannerji. "You do not seem to realize what is at stake here and how cruel these people can be. However —"

The door opened, and Chunder Das came in, followed by one of the seamen carrying a tray, which he set on the floor. There was a large bowl on the tray, which contained a mound of rice covered with meat in a sauce.

"I am afraid that we have no forks or spoons," said Chunder Das. "You will have to eat with your fingers as we do." Then, as they squatted down around the tray, "Well? Have you decided what you are going to do?"

"About what?" asked Andrew, watching Bannerji make a small ball of rice and curry and put it in his mouth.

"Are you going to write a note to your friend Inspector Wyatt as we have asked you to?"

"No," said Sara, making a ball of rice and curry and popping it into her mouth almost as dexterously as Bannerji had.

"No?"

"No," said Andrew.

Frowning, Chunder Das looked at Bannerji, who shrugged and said something to him in Hindustani.

"Very well," said Chunder Das angrily. "*I* will write the note. And if it does not have the desired result — and quickly! — we will take other, more extreme steps!" And he stalked out of the room.

Bannerji said something to the seaman in Hindustani, and the seaman nodded, went out, and came back with a pitcher of water, a basin, and several cups. They all drank thirstily, for the curry was heavily spiced, and after they had eaten they washed their hands in the basin.

The seaman took out the tray, and the three prisoners separated, Bannerji sitting cross-legged and somewhat sulky on a mat against one wall of the almost empty room and Sara and Andrew sitting together against the opposite wall. About a half hour later, Chunder Das came in with an envelope in his hand. There were two of the seamen with him this time and, when Chunder Das said something to them, one of them drew a long knife from a sheath inside the waistband of his trousers and advanced on Sara.

"What are you going to do?" asked Andrew, scrambling to his feet and stationing himself between Sara and the seaman with the knife. The seaman paused, feinted, and when Andrew tried to grapple with him, the other seaman grabbed him from behind and held his arms. With a quick slash, the seaman with the knife cut off a lock of Sara's hair and, at the same time, pulled off one of her hair ribbons.

"This is all we want at the moment," said Chunder Das as the seaman gave him the ribbon and the lock of hair. "We need them so the inspector will know that we are telling the truth when we say that we have you. Next time, if we have to send him something to show that we are in earnest, it will be something that will be a good deal more painful."

"You wouldn't dare!" said Sara, going a little pale.

"Yes, my dear," said Chunder Das quietly. "Yes, we would. You had better accept the fact that there is nothing — but nothing — that we will not do to get what we want!"

There was a strange sound from outside. Ever since they arrived at the house, Andrew and Sara had been aware of sounds from the canal: the hoot of tug whistles, the sound of horses' hoofs on the tow path as they pulled the loaded barges, the calls of the bargemen to one another. But this was different. It sounded like a foghorn, and it was a clear day. Not only that, but there was something familiar about it.

Sara had scrambled to her feet after the lock of her hair had been cut off. Now, more to cover her anxiety than for any other reason, she turned her back on Chunder Das and went over to the window. Andrew went with her. They looked out and, with a start, Sara clutched Andrew's arm, her fingers digging painfully into it.

A small tug was towing a string of six barges east on the canal. Most of them were loaded with coal. But the last barge, which was now just opposite them, was loaded with ashes and broken bricks from one of the dust yards. Whispering Willie, the dustman, stood in the bow of the barge. He had just blown a blast on his foghorn, apparently as a signal of some sort to the tug that was towing them, for it answered with a short whistle. Dropping the foghorn so that it hung from the lanyard around his neck, Willie picked up a shovel and began leveling the ashes in the area around him.

But surprising as this was, this was not what Sara and Andrew were staring at. For sitting in the stern of the barge, wearing a broad-brimmed straw hat and looking quite relaxed as he steered the heavily laden craft, was Beasley!

14

The Chase

When Sara got to her feet, Bannerji got up also, either to protect her as Andrew had tried to do, or to remonstrate with his compatriots. In any case, when the foghorn sounded, he glanced out of the window and reacted as decidedly as Sara and Andrew had, actually saying something in Hindustani under his breath. This made Chunder Das glance out of the window, too, and his reaction was the most violent of all.

When he saw Beasley, his face lit up, and he exclaimed in triumph. He said something to one of the seamen, who ran out of the room, and a moment later a large handbell was rung loudly.

This must have been a signal to the boatyard for, as soon as he heard it, Clemson, the English captain in the peaked cap, came hurrying out of one of the shacks, glanced up at the house and, jumping into the steam launch, blew two answering blasts on its whistle.

There was now a rapid exchange in Hindustani between Chunder Das and Bannerji. Whatever Bannerji said, Chunder Das disagreed with it, for he shook his head impatiently and said to Sara and Andrew, "Come! You will come now, quickly!"

"Where?" asked Sara.

"Onto boat."

"He wants us to come along on the launch," said Bannerji. "I asked him why he could not lock us up if he felt he had to keep us secure, but he said he did not have the time to make sure we were well locked in. He also said, if we came quietly, once they caught Beasley, they would let us go."

"Do you believe him?" asked Andrew.

"I'm not sure. I think he may also want us along so that if anything goes wrong, he may use us as hostages. But, on the whole, I think it is better to go along."

Andrew and Sara exchanged glances. They were not at all certain that they could trust Chunder Das; on the other hand, if they went along in the launch they might be able to help Beasley or escape themselves or both.

"All right," said Sara. "We'll come."

"Quickly, then," said Chundar Das. "Quick, quick!"

He waved his hand, and Sara, Andrew, and Bannerji hurried out of the door, Chunder Das and the seaman bringing up the rear to make sure they did not run away. They hurried down the stairs, and on the floor below, met the other two seamen and Ananda Lal. There was another exchange in Hindustani, and Ananda Lal and one of the seamen led the way out of the back of the house, through the uncared-for garden, and along the path to the boat-yard.

When they got to the launch, a young man in his early twenties was shoveling coal into the glowing furnace, building up the steam pressure, and Clemson was waiting impatiently for them. His eyes widened when he saw Sara and Andrew, and he frowned; but Chunder Das said quickly, "It's all right. They are friends, and they are coming with us."

"All right, then," said Clemson. "Get aboard."

"Back there," said Chunder Das, pointing to the stern of the launch. Sara and Andrew jumped down into the stern of the launch and helped Bannerji to follow. Chunder Das and Ananda Lal got into the bow. The seamen cast off the lines and jumped into the bow also. Clemson advanced the throttle, spun the wheel, and the launch curved from the dock and started up the canal.

There was not as much traffic on the canal as there usually was. A horse plodded along the towpath on the far side, drawing a pair of barges loaded with stone and lumber. On the near side, just past the house they had left, several narrow monkey boats laden with lime and cement were tied up, waiting for a tow. The muddy waters of the canal were stirred as the launch picked up speed to catch the string of barges, which was some distance ahead by now.

The Chase

What would they do when they did catch up, Andrew wondered. For there was no question but that they would. How could a tug towing barges outrun a fast steam launch? And there was no doubt that the launch was fast — as fast as a Thames police launch. Not only that, but Beasley and Whispering Willie did not even seem to realize that they were being chased.

As Andrew wondered if there were any way he could warn them, Clemson blew two short blasts on his whistle to let the man steering the stone and lumber barges know that he was overtaking and passing him.

As the man, a burly bargee in a checked shirt, raised an arm in acknowledgement, Beasley turned and looked back. The sight of the Indians in the bow — for, even at a distance, he could have seen their turbans — must have alarmed him, for sitting up, he called out something to Whispering Willie in the barge's bow. Willie looked back also, then, lifting his horn, he blew a series of short blasts on it. If it was a signal to go faster, it did no good at all. For though the tug towing the barges again answered with a whistle, it did not increase its speed appreciably. In fact, it probably couldn't.

As Beasley, looking worried, kept glancing back, the launch gained rapidly on the barge.

"That the one you're after, the last one?" said Clemson.

"Yes," said Chunder Das.

"What do you want me to do, draw up alongside so you can board her?"

"Yes." He exchanged a few words in Hindustani with one of the seamen. "Up in the front of it — the bow."

The launch drew nearer to the barge. The three seamen were up in the bow. The one who had cut off the lock of Sara's hair had drawn his knife again. A second one had a cosh, a short bludgeon, in his hand. The third had taken the fire axe from its bracket in front of the launch's cabin. Whispering Willie had picked up his shovel and was holding it like a club, prepared to repel boarders.

"How are they going to do it?" asked Sara. "They can't just kidnap Beasley out here on the canal in broad daylight."

"Apparently they think they can," said Andrew. "No one seems to realize what they're doing, and the launch seems to be very fast — faster than anything else around here at the moment."

"They may be in for more trouble than they think. Whispering Willie looks as if he's going to fight, and I've a feeling that Beasley will, too." Then, lowering her voice, "Isn't there anything we can do to help?"

"There may be," said Andrew quietly. "Let's wait and see."

The launch was up level with the barge now. One of the Indians waved his hand. Clemson spun the wheel, and the launch swung in at the bow of the barge. Raising the axe, the Indian brought it down on the barge's bow, cutting through the tow line. Almost at once the barge began losing way, slowing up, while the tug and the other barges drew away from it. Clemson spun his wheel the other way, and the launch started to circle around behind the barge, where the Indians could make fast and board her.

Beasley threw the barge's helm over and, with what momentum it had left, the barge swung toward a warehouse on the north bank of the canal. Its inertia carried it forward until it bumped against the piles of the dock on the canal side of the warehouse. With seamanlike agility, Willie threw the barge's hawser around one of the piles and pulled it tight to hold the barge in place. Then he picked up his shovel again. Beasley, meanwhile, had picked up a boathook, which he prepared to use as a pike.

Clemson brought the launch alongside the barge at its middle, and two of the seamen jumped on board and advanced on Willie in the bow while Chunder Das, Ananda Lal, and the third seaman climbed up and went toward Beasley in the stern. The two Indian seamen, one with his knife and the other with the axe, began circling Willie, wary of his shovel and his determined expression. Chunder Das and his white-robed companion each had a length of silken cord in his hand, either to use as a noose to strangle Beasley with or to tie him up once he had been subdued.

Bannerji had moved forward and was standing on the launch's gunwale, watching what was happening with great intensity.

"Now?" whispered Sara.

"Don't," said Clemson just as quietly. "Stay on board here and don't interfere."

As Andrew glanced at him, surprised by the friendliness in his voice, several things happened. The Indian with the axe struck at Willie, and he fended off the blow with the shovel, brought it around, and knocked down the Indian with the knife. Chunder Das, Ananda Lal, and the third seaman moved in on Beasley, and the warehouse doors opened with a crash and out ran eight or ten police constables, led by Sergeant Tucker and followed by Inspector Wyatt.

What followed could not be called a struggle. Taken completely by surprise and overwhelmed by superior numbers, the five Indians were subdued and handcuffed before they even realized what was happening.

Beasley now turned to look at Bannerji.

"Well, look who's here," he said cheerfully. "My Indian friend as ever was. Would you like to come aboard, old bean?"

Bannerji, almost as dazed as his compatriots, looked at them and then at Beasley.

"What?" he said. "I suppose so."

Beasley held out his boathook and pulled Bannerji up on to the barge. Whispering Willie, meanwhile, had dropped his shovel and strolled toward them. Reaching Bannerji, he said something — not in his usual whisper, but in a clear, normal voice — and not in English, but in Hindustani.

The effect was electric — as sudden and astonishing as what had happened when the warehouse doors had burst open.

"You?" said Bannerji, stiffening. "You mean it is you?"

With a motion that was almost too swift to follow, he pulled a silk scarf from inside his belt, and with that same motion whipped it around Willie's neck. (Andrew remembered later what he had said about the *rumal* — how silver coins were knotted into one corner of the sacred scarf to weight it so that it could be used in just this way.) Pulling the scarf tight, Bannerji turned his knuckles in to draw it even tighter.

"*Jai Kali!*" he shouted. "*Jai Bhowani!*"

With that, Andrew realized that though Bannerji might have seemed soft and overweight, he was a tremendously powerful man.

Tucker and several of the constables ran forward to rescue Willie, but Willie held up his hand to stop them. For a moment, several moments, they stood there face to face: Bannerji using all his great strength to pull the scarf tighter around Willie's bandaged neck and either break it or strangle him, and Willie standing there quietly, calmly, as if urging him to do his worst. Then, as Bannerji's efforts began to slacken, as his mouth opened and his eyes widened in disbelief, Willie turned slightly, raised one arm and brought it down to break Bannerji's grip, then with a sudden movement, tripped him so that he fell backward on the barge's ashes.

"All right, sergeant," he said to Tucker. "I'll take your darbies now."

Tucker, his own eyes wide in surprise, passed over the handcuffs, and, bending down, Willie snapped them on Bannerji's wrists.

"And that," he said, getting up and dusting the ashes from his hands, "seems to be that." He turned, looking curiously at Wyatt, who had not said a word since the police had come running out of the warehouse. "Is anything wrong, inspector?"

"A great deal," said Wyatt, glaring at Sara and Andrew. "What the blazes are the two of you doing here?"

15

The Deceivers

"But it wasn't our fault," said Sara.

"Of course not," said Wyatt scathingly. "You were on board the launch for a tour of the canal system, which leaves London Bridge every hour on the hour!"

"You're being sarcastic because you're angry," said Andrew patiently, "but it really wasn't our fault. We were on the launch because we'd been kidnapped."

"Kidnapped where and when?"

"At Beasley's shop this morning."

"What were you doing there?"

"Looking for Sean."

"Why?"

Andrew hesitated, glancing at Sara. They were standing just outside the warehouse — he, Sara, Wyatt, Beasley, and, somewhat surprisingly, Captain Clemson. The reason he hesitated was that Wyatt might have a right to be angry at this point.

And then, again surprisingly, Clemson spoke up. "Excuse me, inspector," he said. "I don't want to interfere, but they *weren't* on the launch of their own free will. The Indians had them in the house and brought them along."

"Is he a friend of yours?" Sara asked Wyatt, looking at Clemson.

"In a way," said Wyatt. "But he seems to be a friend of yours, too, trying to find excuses for your being in a place where you shouldn't have been."

"Look, we all know why you're so angry, inspector," said Beasley. "It's because you like this pair of rapscallions — as who doesn't — and you were worried about them. But I suspect things wouldn't have worked out as nicely as they did if it wasn't for them. I'll bet they were the ones who spotted us from the house."

"You don't say! And what do you want me to do about it — give them each a medal?"

"No," said Andrew, playing on the fact that Wyatt was speaking a little more moderately. "All we want is for you not to be quite so angry with us."

"And of course let us know what's been going on," said Sara. "Exactly what's been happening and why."

"You *would* want to know that," said Wyatt dryly. "And you'll remember everything I say, and the next time it'll be even harder to keep you out of any case you get within a mile of."

"No, it won't," said Andrew.

"Yes, it will. I'm not saying that the two of you aren't smart and useful. What I am saying is that Beasley's right. I do worry about you, and this case was dangerous, more dangerous than any you have been involved in. Still . . . all right. Come on inside and we'll go over things."

He opened a door and led them into the warehouse, which was empty except for a few scattered crates and bales. The large, sliding door on the opposite side that led to the street was open, and Sergeant Tucker was standing there, supervising as the handcuffed Indians were loaded into a black police van. When it left, he closed the door and joined them. All of them, Clemson and Beasley included, walked toward a sink where Whispering Willie was washing the dust and dirt from his hands and face. He turned as they approached and, although he was still wearing his dustman's clothes, he no longer had on his fantail hat and without it, he looked completely different; not just cleaner, but more intelligent and alert.

"I'd like to introduce two young people whom, I believe, you've already met," said Wyatt. "Sara Wiggins and Andrew Tillett. Captain Ian Ross, formerly of the Punjab Rifles and later of the Indian Criminal Investigation Department."

"Yes, we have already met," said Willie, smiling. "But of course I'm delighted to meet you both again under happier and more salubrious circumstances."

"Thank you," said Sara. "Then you're Mr. X?"

"I beg your pardon?"

"The British agent who penetrated the Thugs' organization and helped destroy it," said Andrew. "At least, that's what Bannerji called you when he told us about you."

"He told you about me, did he? Yes, he would. And I suppose I am the man he called Mr. X. At least, I'm the man he and his friends have been looking for."

"It's all pretty confusing," said Sara. "There were times when I rather liked him — Bannerji, I mean — and times when I didn't. But now . . . well, am I right in thinking he was a Thug, too?"

"Not just *a* Thug, but the leader, the brains, of the small group that was left — the most dangerous group of all, and the one that the Indian government asked Scotland Yard to find and capture. And yes, it is all rather confusing. Perhaps the best thing to do is to tell the whole story from the beginning."

"I wish you would," said Wyatt. "While I know some of it and have guessed still more, there's a good deal I don't know."

"I find that hard to believe," said Captain Ross. "You seem to have done a remarkable job of foreseeing everything that happened and preparing for it. Still. . . . As the inspector told you," he said to Sara and Andrew, "my name is Ross, and I come of an old Anglo-Indian family."

"Meaning that you were born in India?" said Andrew.

"Yes. My father came to India as a very young man

with a commission in the Punjab Rifles, married the colonel's daughter, and later became a district commissioner. Though I came back to England and was educated here, during my early years I learned Hindustani, Urdu, and several other dialects from the Indians who were part of our household. And so I was particularly well qualified for the role I was to play later on."

"How were you selected?" asked Wyatt.

"I wasn't selected. A good friend of my father's was on the viceroy's staff. He knew of my knowledge of Indian languages and customs; and when the Thugs became active again, he asked if I would be willing to do what Captain Sleemen had done, penetrate the organization in disguise and help to destroy it. I knew something about the horrors for which the Thugs had been responsible — the parents and sister of an Indian officer who served in the Rifles with me had been killed by them — so I agreed."

"I gather you were successful," said Andrew.

"Not I, we, for I wasn't alone. A Muslim constable from the CID named Amir Ali worked with me from the beginning, and whatever we accomplished, we did together. I won't go into the details of how we got the evidence we wanted. The fact is that we did. There was a new series of trials, and it was clear that the organization had again been effectively smashed. But Amir Ali and I were convinced that there were a few high-ranking Thugs still at large, men we had never been able to identify. And we finally got word from an informer that such men not only existed, but had sworn to find out who we were and take vengeance on us."

"They had no idea who you were?" said Sara.

"No. Our identities had been carefully protected. But the Indian government was unwilling to take any chances, so they gave us both an extended leave and suggested that we go to England for a time while other members of the CID tried to find out who these men were who were determined to kill us."

"Wasn't the fact that you were leaving India apt to make them suspicious?" asked Wyatt.

"We hoped not," said Captain Ross. "My brother had been in the Indian service, too, and had been invalided home about a year before with relapsing fever. He had just died, and the leave was ostensibly given to me to go home and help settle his estate. I left on a P & O boat. Amir Ali, traveling second class, left on the same boat, supposedly to do some work with the East India Company in London. We carefully avoided one another, acted as if we did not know one another. But someone either knew or guessed the truth about Amir Ali. He went ashore when we stopped at Alexandria and did not return. He was found strangled in an alley."

"Isn't it possible that he was killed by a robber?" asked Andrew.

"No," said Ross. "A note pinned to his chest said, 'The vengeance of Bhowani on all who betray her.' I did not find that out until later, but I did not need to know it. As soon as I heard he was dead, I knew who had killed him and decided I couldn't trust anyone to protect me and I'd better disappear."

"We were fairly sure that that's what you'd done," said Wyatt. "What we weren't sure of was how you'd done it."

"I left the boat and went to France as a Swedish engineer," said Ross. "I traveled through France and entered England as a French archeologist, back from Cambodia, and going to London to do some work at the British Museum."

"But you still didn't come to the Yard," said Wyatt.

"No. Though I have the greatest respect for you in ordinary criminal matters, I didn't think you knew enough about Indians to be able to handle this. So I decided to continue on my own. Or at least without official help, but with that of your good friend Beasley."

He turned and bowed to him, and Beasley bowed back.

"How did you get to him?" asked Sara.

"When my father returned to England some years ago, he met Beasley and they became friends. When Father died, Beasley sold some of his Indian artifacts for my mother. She wrote me about him, speaking very warmly of him, and so did my brother when he got to London. He sounded like the kind of person who could help me, so I went to him, told him who I was, and what my problem was and what I needed."

"You mean you wanted him to help you create an identity that would keep you safe," said Wyatt.

"Exactly. He told me about you and said he was sure you could handle the Thugs. But, since you were away at the moment, he suggested I go into hiding until you returned. We discussed several possible identities, but when he suggested that of a dustman, I felt that was ideal for several reasons."

"I think I know one of the reasons," said Andrew impulsively.

"What's that?" asked Captain Ross.

"In India a dustman is an Untouchable, which means that most Indians — Hindus, anyway — would avoid you, keep as far away from you as possible."

"Very good! How did you happen to think of that?"

"I remember Bannerji's reaction — how he drew back — the first time he met you."

"While we're at it, I think I know why you pretended you had a sore throat and talked in a whisper," said Sara. "Wasn't it because you weren't sure of your Cockney accent and slang?"

"Well, well," said Ross approvingly. "Were they always this perceptive?" he asked Wyatt. "Or did they become this way through their association with you?"

"A little of each," said Wyatt. "But go on with your story."

"One thing I'm not clear about," said Andrew, "is how

the Indians came to suspect that Beasley knew the man they were looking for."

"We're not positive," said Ross, "but Beasley and I think it may have begun with that statue of Kali."

"Was that the one you had in your shop?" Sara asked Beasley. "The one that Sean hated and that you finally took home and hid?"

"Yes," said Beasley. "It belonged to Captain Ross's brother, and his wife didn't like it either. When his brother died several months ago, his widow gave it to me to sell. Eventually, I put it in the window, but when Captain Ross came to the shop, he told me about Kali's connection with the Thugs and advised me to get rid of it. I did, but in the meantime Bannerji saw it. He knew that the man he was looking for had to be an Anglo-Indian and, looking for an Indian connection, he probably went to the British Museum and asked them for the names of anyone interested in Indian art or artifacts. They had originally given my name to Captain Ross's father and now they gave it to Bannerji, very likely telling him how useful I had been to the old man. Bannerji came to the shop, saw the statue and that must have made him decide there was something worth pursuing there."

"We think that at that point he probably checked back," said Captain Ross, "and realized that we — a Ross father and two Ross sons — could be the Anglo-Indian family he had been looking for. Then he found that, although I had left India supposedly to help my sister-in-law settle my brother's estate, I had never arrived here. That must have made him fairly sure that I was the man he wanted and that Beasley had helped create a new identity for me. So he had his fellow Thugs — Chunder Das and the others — use every trick he and they could think of to get Beasley to tell them what they wanted to know."

"That was what he was trying to do when he wanted to hypnotize you, wasn't it?" Andrew asked Beasley. And when Beasley nodded, "I thought so. That was when I first began to become suspicious of him. But what happened when we thought you were sick? Was it because of some kind of drug as Dr. Reeves thought?"

"It was," said Wyatt. "One of the first things I did when I heard what had happened was to ask Reeves to go to Beasley's house and see if he could find what had been giving him that terrible anxiety and those frightening hallucinations. And he did find it — in the tea Beasley had been drinking."

"My tea?" said Beasley.

"Yes. It was a drug made of spoiled rye and other grain that is sometimes used as a poison and sometimes to cause hallucinations. When the Thugs decided to go to work on you they must have gotten into your house somehow and mixed it with your tea."

"I can understand why I felt better when I left the house then," said Beasley. "But why did I feel worse when you moved me from hospital to Andrew's house?"

"Because somehow and at some point Bannerji substituted more of the drug for the medicine that Dr. Reeves had prescribed for you."

"It must have been when he brought you that Mogul painting," said Andrew. "If you remember, he bumped into the night table, almost knocked it over. And after that we all spent some time looking at the painting."

"Of course," said Beasley. "That's probably one of the reasons he wanted me out of hospital, so no one would notice that the bottle had been changed. And of course he wanted to give me more of the drug so I'd agree to let him hypnotize me."

"Exactly."

"Though we followed your instructions this morning," said Captain Ross to Wyatt, "and Beasley wasn't the least bit surprised that you had a plan of action ready so quickly, I must confess that I was. Will you tell us how you worked it out?"

"First of all, we spent a lot more time on our planning than you think," said Wyatt. "As soon as you left India, we received a note from the CID telling us what you had done, why you were coming to England, and asking us to look out for you. When you disappeared in Alexandria, we got a second message telling us about that and about the death of Amir Ali. We realized at once why you had disappeared — that you knew the Thugs were after you — and had decided to come to England in disguise. I was given the job of finding and protecting you and — if possible — catching and nobbling our friends, the Thugs. Unfortunately, your return came at an awkward time for me."

"Awkward?" said Ross, puzzled. Then his face cleared. "Of course. You were getting married, going away on your honeymoon."

"Right. I discussed the matter with my chief, and he pointed out that there was no way we could tell when you were going to show up here. It might be in days, but it might not be for weeks or months. He insisted that I go ahead with my plans — after, of course, making any arrangements here that I thought might be useful."

"That's what interests me. What arrangements did you make?"

"One was to make sure that Sergeant Tucker knew where I was at all times. He was familiar with the case, knew what was involved, and had instructions to bring me back whenever it seemed necessary. Another very important element was bringing in Inspector Clemson of the Thames Police."

"I suspected that he was an ally even before he came in here with you and Beasley," said Ross, smiling at him.

"As I said, a very important one," said Wyatt. "We knew that if — Heaven forbid! — our Indian friends should accomplish their mission, they would want to leave England quickly and secretly. The best way to do this would be to take a boat downriver and pick up a ship at Gravesend or out in the Channel, avoiding the regular ports. So Inspector Clemson posed as the skipper of a fast launch who was not fastidious about its use, the implication being that he was a smuggler. Word of this was passed to all the boatmen in the area, who were asked to refer any Indians who tried to hire them to him. A few days ago he let the Yard know that he had been approached and hired."

"That was by Chunder Das and company, I take it."

"It was."

"Why didn't you arrest them right away?" asked Sara.

"Because, while we were fairly sure that they were the Indians we were looking for, we had to be certain of it *and* we had to catch them doing something criminal. More important, we weren't sure that the men who had hired Inspector Clemson were *all* there were. I suspected that their chief, the brains of the group, was not with them."

"Bannerji."

"Right. But even with all our planning, I'm not sure things would have worked out as well as they did if it weren't for several surprising strokes of luck."

"What were they?" asked Andrew.

"One of them, naturally, was that we were in on things from the beginning," said Sara, grinning.

"You're joking," said Wyatt, "and I shouldn't admit it because I was ready to have you keelhauled when I saw you in that launch, but . . . you're right. When I got back here, you gave me information that it would have taken me quite a while to put together from regular sources. I was able to deduce from what you told me that Whispering Willie was Captain Ross and deduce further that he had helped Beasley escape from your house and was probably hiding him at the dust yard where he himself was living. This was confirmed by a telegram Beasley sent me."

"That was the telegram you got at the Yard?" said Andrew.

"Yes. Another bit of luck was the fact that our Indian friends had taken a house right on the canal. They had done it to be close to Captain Clemson when they wanted to escape; but it gave me the chance to make use of the device that I did — trolling for them the way a fisherman does when he trails a whiting behind his boat to catch a mackerel."

"Can I ask one more question?" asked Andrew.

" 'I've answered three questions and that is enough,' " said Wyatt with mock ferocity. "Do you know what comes after that?"

"Of course," said Andrew, who had known his *Alice in Wonderland* before he knew his multiplication tables. " 'Do you think I can listen all day to such stuff? Be off or I'll kick you downstairs.' But I'm not asking it of you. I'd like to ask it of Captain Ross."

"Of course, Andrew," said the captain.

"What did you say to Bannerji that made him try to strangle you?"

"Well, I was fairly sure he was the man we wanted —
the chief Thug — and of course he didn't know that I
was the man *he'd* been looking for. So I said in Hindustani, 'Well, friend, either you mistook the signs' —
Thugs sacrifice to Bhowani before they do anything in
her name and only proceed if the omens are favorable —
'or else she has failed you.' That told him who I was.
What *he* shouted when he threw his strangling scarf
around my neck — Jai Bhowani! — meant Victory to
Bhowani."

"That brings me to my last question," said Sara. "How
is it that he didn't — *couldn't* — strangle you. He certainly
tried hard enough."

"He did. And under ordinary circumstances he would
have broken my neck. But that was something I had prepared for from the beginning." He held up a long and
very dirty bandage. "Do you remember this?"

"Yes. You had it around your throat. Because, you said,
you had a quinsy."

"That's right. You guessed before that I pretended I
had a sore throat and talked in a whisper because I wasn't
sure about my Cockney accent. That was true. But there
was another reason. Under the bandage, I had this." He
held up a wide strip of leather reinforced with steel. "This
leather collar would protect my neck against anything
short of the guillotine."

"The Deceivers," said Andrew thoughtfully. "Isn't
that what the Thugs were called?"